M000188743

The Carnival Chemist and Other Stories

Bruce Kirkpatrick

Also by Bruce Kirkpatrick

Fiction

Hard Left

The Resurrection of Johnny Roe

Non-Fiction

Lumberjack Jesus: How to Develop Faith Despite Pitfalls, Roadblocks, Stupidity, and Prejudice

Dedication

For Heather

Acknowledgments

Muchas gracias, Tucson, Arizona. I've traveled to this lovely city near the Mexican border regularly for fifty years. On a recent two-week trip, I perched in a comfy chair and let the splendor of the Santa Catalina Mountains envelop and inspire me. I scribbled madly with a No. 2 pencil each morning, filling a yellow pad as these stories tumbled out.

Thank you to the men, women, and couples who have shared their lives with me. These stories are complete fabrications of my imagination. So, if you see yourself or your situation in here anywhere, I hope you'll realize that these are universal stories that can happen to any of us at any time. In one way or another, several have touched me and my family. None of us are immune to tragedy, joy, or the radiance of the spirit.

Virginia McCullough deserves a round of praise for the way she edits my scribblings, especially as she helps me develop my female characters. I know men well, but I'm still learning about women.

The "Heather" from the Dedication page is my daughter-in-law, Heather Sweeney Kirkpatrick, who is not only a wonderful mom to my grandkids, but also a lawyer extraordinaire. She guided me through the intricacies of the law in the story of *The Carnival Chemist.* Of course, laws change, and even though the story is set in 2015, any omissions or mistakes are all on me.

I couldn't do this work without the love, laughter, and patience of my wife, Nancy.

As always, thank you, Jesus.

Table of Contents

Book One

LIVING

Every Wednesday

It was Wednesday evening, and I was hiding out in my room. I felt sick to my stomach, but I always felt that way on Wednesdays. I watched out my window for our rusty old Pontiac to pull into the muddy lanes that we called our driveway. I glanced at the clock, 5:37 p.m. The call from the kitchen would be coming soon.

My dad always visited the bar on Wednesdays. He got off early that day and could settle in to visit his buddies at the bar earlier than usual. That doesn't mean he didn't visit the bar on other days, but he didn't stay long on those days. He knew dinner was served at six, so he'd have a drink or two before heading home.

But not Wednesdays. He tended to lose track of time that day.

I stayed in my room and pretended to study my math book, but all these new word problems made my eyes glaze. Addition, subtraction, multiplication—yep, I could pick those up. But when somebody started throwing words into math problems, I started to sink. I didn't blame my teacher, Mrs. Scott. Most of the time, her heart wasn't in it. Most of the kids had heard the rumors about Mr. Scott leaving her, and that only meant one thing—divorce. Nobody had been divorced in our town since the Petersons, and that was only because the Peterson girl had got herself pregnant and the parents couldn't agree on what to do. I never heard what happened to the girl, but that was a long time ago. I'm only ten now, so I probably wouldn't have understood. At least that's what Mom said when things got complicated. She might be right, but every once in a while, I wanted to at least try to figure things out.

But I had bigger worries than math or Mrs. Scott's divorce.

I had closed my door so I could claim that I didn't hear Mom when she called me. But she wouldn't let me play my transistor radio during homework time, so I couldn't use that excuse.

Then a knock on the door. Mom said she was teaching me proper manners, so she would never have just opened the door without knocking. She learned that one from Dad. He said boys needed their privacy. I didn't know what I needed privacy for, but I was glad for manners.

She stuck her head in the open doorway. "Robert, please go down to the bar and tell your father it's time to come home." That never changed. She said the exact same words every Wednesday.

She usually called me Bobby, but on Wednesdays, I was Robert. It sounded more grown-up. And I guess I did feel a little more like an adult on Wednesdays, but I wasn't sure I liked it.

"Aww, Mom, do I have to?" I blurted in a whiny voice like I always did. But I was pretty sure, once you hit ten years old, whining didn't work anymore.

She didn't bother to answer that, just holding her stare a few seconds longer, one eyebrow raised.

"But it's dark out, and it could be dangerous."

"You've done that walk many, many times, sweetie. You know it's not a bit dangerous. Just dress warm because it's cold. And you may have to walk back."

I tried a few more excuses in my head—I'd been jotting them down instead of tackling the "if Johnny leaves home and home is 12 miles away…" problem in my math book. But I knew they weren't any use.

My last resort was a huge sigh and a sad look at my mom, but she'd already left the room.

I dragged myself to the alcove inside the back door and searched for my galoshes—I knew she wouldn't let me leave without them—and my beanie. My boots fit over my shoes and came up past my ankles. I flipped over the metal latches that held the boots together. Then I buttoned up my coat and said, "What if he's not there?"

"Then we'll all be pleasantly surprised, won't we? Tell him to come right home. Get a move on, buster." Calling me buster meant the discussion was over and I needed to get moving. I tried not to slam the door as I left. I'd hear about it when I got home if I did.

It had snowed earlier in the day but only a few inches. I walked in the street along the curb when I didn't see any cars, like I was trudging through deep drifts, kicking up clumps of snow. Some jumped the top of my boots and caught in the cuffs of my pants and soon I'd have wet feet. The worst. But I was already feeling miserable, so I didn't much care.

I don't know how far that bar was from home, but it seemed like miles. Like six. I had to go four or five blocks down to the center of town, turn right on Main Street, and then walk all the way past Fourth Avenue. The snow wasn't as pretty down here, all slushy and dirty from the cars, so I stuck to the sidewalks. The misty air, with a few flurries mixed in, got caught in the streetlights and made light on the snow a weird yellow.

From blocks away, I could see Lucky's bright sign blinking on and off. I noticed that they had gotten the letter K fixed in the light. For the longest time, it said LUC-Y'S, and I thought the bar was named after some girl. But my dad had corrected me. No right-thinking man would name a bar after a girl cuz bars didn't attract too many girls and if you named it a girl's name then it was probably trying to attract girls.

Finally, I got to the bar. I stood at the door and tried to talk myself into opening it.

The bar was mysterious to me. Some of it scary, some like I just didn't know, like a problem you'd try and figure out. Dad always said I had plenty of time to catch on, so I stopped asking. When adults tell you that you'll figure it out when you get older, and you don't even know what you have to figure out, worrying doesn't do much good. I was too busy worrying about math and word problems and, every once in a while, Mrs. Scott.

I took a deep breath and swung the door open. To the left I saw a row of booths, each with a man and a woman, mostly sitting close together.

Then I got hit with the smoke. I think everyone in that place had a cigarette. I always could tell when my dad had been at the bar, whether it was a Wednesday or not, because I could smell that reek on his clothes.

Right inside the door there was a popcorn machine. I stopped and took a deep whiff.

The bar had red-topped stools with metal legs. When heads swiveled toward me, I was sure my face matched the red on top of the stools. A couple of men—they were all men on the stools—nodded like they knew me, and one motioned with his thumb toward the back of the bar.

Before I saw my dad, Geno, the guy behind the bar, leaned over and said, "Hey, Bobby, how's it hangin'?" That got a big laugh from a couple of men. But Geno's smile turned sour, as if somebody didn't like what I thought was a joke on me. But I didn't really know. Sometimes when people laughed, I didn't know any better whether to laugh or not. Sometimes it really sucks being a kid.

Then my dad leaned out into the aisle and caught my eye. I hurried to him and came alongside his right leg, anchored on the floor. He gently took my beanie off my head and handed it to me. I had forgotten—no hats on inside. Then he fluffed my hair.

He looked down at me, but I averted my eyes. I only looked down at his galoshes. He had the small ones on today, the ones that barely covered the bottom of his shoes and came up barely over the soles. He was wearing one of his suits, so I knew he'd been with customers. I didn't know what he sold or what customers were, but I knew that on a Wednesday, if he had a suit on, he'd been with them. His gray hat sat on the bar beside his beer next to a tiny glass. I never knew what was so special that they only gave you such a tiny glass of it.

"Mom send you?" He didn't say it like it was much of a question.

I nodded.

"Be ready in a second." He turned back toward the bar, keeping his hand on my shoulder. "You want a cherry coke?"

I shook my head. Yes, I desperately wanted one, but I wanted to keep to Mom's schedule even more.

"One for the road, Bob?" Geno yelled from down the bar, holding up a bottle with a tiny little spout on the end of it. I had my dad's name, or he had mine, or we had each other's.

"Naw, my escort has arrived," he said back. "My carriage awaits."

I'd been called an escort before but never a carriage.

I let my eyes drift to the other men at the bar. My dad was the only one wearing a suit and tie. The other men had on sweatshirts or sweaters. A couple had uniforms, one in dark green, the other in dark blue, with sweatshirts underneath the short sleeve shirts.

As he finished his beer and stood up to go, Dad got several pats on the back and waves from the men at the bar. He grabbed his hat and perched it on the back of his head.

"Let's go, bud," he said, steering my head toward the front door. When we got outside, he shivered and almost lost his balance on the icy patch near the door. He reached out to me, grabbed my shoulder, and steadied himself.

"I parked over there." He pointed to the side parking lot.

When my dad was with his customers, he drove to work. I had forgotten that because most other times he walked. He searched in his long black winter coat for his keys, slipping a few more times as we crossed the icy lot toward the Pontiac, all the time his hand on my shoulder.

I didn't like Dad driving when he'd been at the bar, but I didn't know what to say or do to stop him. He fumbled with the keys and tried to insert the wrong one before muttering under his breath. He let out a large belch, and I caught the smell of beer when we finally got the door open and we got inside. He inched out of the lot. As we headed down Fourth, I had an idea.

"Boy, it's pretty icy out. Maybe we should just walk home, huh?"

He looked over at me with a squinty stare and shook his head. "I got it."

After a few more blocks, he belched again and turned to me. "You scared?" he asked.

"A little, I guess."

"Why?"

I scrunched my shoulders and shook my head.

He waited, still looking at me.

"It's Wednesday, and you've been at the bar a long time, that's all," I said.

"How do you know how long I've been there? You some kind of mind reader?"

He slowed down and pulled over to the curb. "But you're right," he said, almost a whisper.

We sat there, not saying anything. Finally, he smiled and said, "You drive."

I had nothing, no reply. My mouth just hung open.

"What?!" I said.

He shrugged. "Yeah, you're almost old enough, and who's going to know."

"I...I...can't even reach the pedals."

"Oh, right." He frowned first, but then he smiled

"Just come on over," he said, motioning me toward him, his right arm extended and welcoming.

I didn't move.

"You can help me. Come on, nobody's going to know." His fingers kept on beckoning me. He grabbed my arm and tugged.

I slid onto his lap, and as he pulled away from the curb, I noticed that his hands weren't on the steering wheel. Just hovering in midair, out to the sides, like a runner crossing the finish line in a race.

"You're driving," he said, motioning with one hand toward the steering wheel.

I gripped the wheel and pulled it hard left.

"Easy, easy." He nudged the wheel back to the center of the road with his right hand. "Just make small little corrections." The word *corrections* came out of his mouth weird, like "corrations" or something. But I didn't have time to worry it because suddenly he gunned it.

I couldn't look at the speedometer, but I knew we were moving. And fast. His laugh filled the car, and I smelled beer again.

"Keep her steady now, keep her steady," Dad said, his voice rising against the roar of the engine. He slowed a little as we went through the stoplight. I think it was green, but I couldn't really be sure. I was caught somewhere between not wanting to wet my pants and being really excited. Dad gunned it again.

I kept moving the wheel, right, then left, then right again with small little corrections Dad showed me when he nudged my arms to go one way or the other. I caught on to the rhythm, and we flew up Main Street. I don't remember making the turn off of Fourth.

He honked the horn a couple of times, like saying "get out of the way" or "look at us." I didn't know which. Didn't really care either.

When he slowed and then stopped at a red light, I was breathing fast, and my heart was pumping like I'd been running.

"Fun, huh?" he said.

I nodded, but I was done. I pushed at his right arm to escape.

"Had enough?"

"Yeah, you can take it from here," I said, sliding back to my side.

He didn't have to tell me not to tell Mom. I smiled at him, and he smiled back. We had a secret.

When the light changed, he drove the rest of the way home,

barely inching along. I couldn't smell beer anymore.

He pulled up to the muddy tracks of our driveway and parked by the garage. He turned off the engine but didn't get out of the car. He just sighed and looked off toward someplace.

"Are you ever going to divorce Mom?" I asked, finally breaking the silence after a few moments.

"What? No, we love each other. What brought that on?"

"That's what all the kids are saying about Mrs. Scott."

"Your teacher, that Mrs. Scott?"

"Yeah."

He thought for a while. "Well, maybe the Scotts are having trouble. Or maybe they don't love each other anymore. I don't know them very well. And I'd be careful about spreading rumors. That's not a nice thing to do."

He was trying to change the subject. "But you and Mom love each other still?"

"Of course, we do, bud. Very much."

"I don't think she loves you as much on Wednesdays."

He turned toward me and looked like he was thinking hard about it. "Maybe not, but she still loves me. And if I only get her love six out of seven days, that's way better than most folks I know. I'll take it."

We sat in the car another few minutes. This was either another time when I didn't know what was going on or I was too young to know better. But I didn't think it was either. I think it was a time for me to grow up. Even if I didn't want to.

"Hey, who knows, maybe she loves me even more on Wednesdays. That's possible, isn't it, bud?"

"I'm probably too young to figure that out. But I don't think so."

"Just so you know," my dad said. As he leaned in closer to me, I caught that smell of beer again. "I appreciate you looking out for me. And me and Mom. Just between us guys. Got it?"

"Sure," I managed.

"Besides, we're Catholic. Father Bernard would never let us

get away with divorce. Never gonna happen."

We got out of the car and headed inside. I noticed my socks were wet, but I didn't care. I grabbed my dad's hand, and we walked up the back stairs.

I didn't know what being Catholic had to with anything, but it didn't make me feel any better about Wednesdays.

Becoming Visible

I wouldn't have been self-conscious in front of the male dermatologist as he surveyed my naked body except that the assistant taking notes was a young woman, Brittany.

After he finished—no bad spots, yeah—I pulled the hospital gown back around me.

"Now let's look at your face," he said. He followed with a series of head nods and concerned looks as he took off his designer glasses to get a closer look.

"I'd like to freeze a few of those—right here...and here—just because they look a little pre-cancerous."

"What's that mean?" I asked.

"Well, I take this little machine, there'll be a little pain..."

"No, I mean the pre-cancerous part."

"Oh, nothing to worry about, and I don't even want to biopsy them. They're probably just sun-damaged spots, and it's precautionary that we take care of them now. Before they turn cancerous."

"Oh," I said without much conviction.

"This will leave a scab," he said, pointing to a small metal bottle that looked like a miniature can of hair spray. "At your age, they should last a week, maybe two. Are you okay with that?"

My age?

A few friends had the scabby look on their faces when they visited a dermatologist, so I knew what he meant.

"Or we could schedule it for a later time if you want to check your schedule."

"No, we can do it today," I said.

After the procedure—and don't let anybody tell you it doesn't hurt—he settled back in his chair, smiling at me.

"Anything else?" he asked.

"One thing," I replied. "What can you do with this"—I circled my hand around my 67-year-old face—"cuz I have my fiftieth high school reunion next summer? Can you take twenty years off?"

He smiled and leaned forward, reengaged in my care. "No, but I can do ten easy."

"Yeah? How?"

"Oh, I love this part," he beamed. "Botox. I can fill in around here," pointing to my crow's-feet, "although some men like to leave those, and just concentrate on the lines on your forehead. They're rather deeply etched."

He didn't give me much time to ask questions. He was on a roll.

"It lasts three or four months and, in the scheme of things, not expensive at all. We sell each unit for $13, and if I did your forehead, right here, that'd be about fifteen to twenty units. Maybe each eye, if you do decide to go all the way, another ten or so units for each eye. It's really the best, most logical approach, no pain, in and out with an office visit, you look terrific all summer, and there're no long-term consequences," he concluded, smiling up at me.

"Okay, I'll think about it, thanks."

"Sure. Just let us know, and we can get it on the schedule. And it beats taking a trophy wife to the reunion," he said, chuckling to himself. "Brittiany will finish up. Let's check those in six months." Then he slipped out the door.

As she filled out the chart, I looked at her, willing her to say something about the "trophy wife" comment.

She avoided my eyes but said, "He's not married," as if that was all she was going to say on the subject.

But the seed had been planted.

I wasn't married either.

As I drove home, I wondered, what exactly is a trophy wife?

Somebody you're proud of, somebody who is new and shiny, like a trophy, somebody who was awarded to you…like from the gods above…for a life well lived. Somebody like that?

But I'd never been very good with women. Dated several, two seriously but never so seriously that they considered marrying me. And after all, I'd never asked either one. I didn't have any prospects on the immediate horizon.

Why would I want to impress my high school classmates anyway with a trophy wife? Or a wife at all?

Because I was invisible in high school. I had a few close buddies, but mostly I was a loner. I never dated. Never. Missed the proms, the drive-in movies, the late-night cuddle sessions. No kissy-face, honeybunch. I never joined a sports team or an academic team, not even Spanish Club. I made no attempt to join anything.

I ventured directly from high school to Vietnam. Re-upped for a second tour. Kept my head down and my feet dry—and made it out alive. Then I became even more reclusive. Sometimes even my parents lost track of me as I wandered the country from job to job. Not bad jobs. Good jobs, actually. I got some tech training in the Army and discovered I had a knack for it.

I never went to college, but that didn't matter to me and didn't hinder my job prospects. I picked up on computers early and just sort of found my way around. Took as many courses and seminars as I could—making my employer pay for most of them—and worked my way up the pay scale. Since I had no encumbrances, like a wife or kids, I did okay. Saved some money, bought new cars, lived pretty well.

For some reason I can't even remember today, I went back for my ten-year reunion. Most people gave me blank stares and wondered who I was. They'd sneak a peek at the high-school photo of me on the badge pinned to my chest, then look up at me, and the blank stare became blanker. A healthy weight gain, long hair, and a beard helped camouflage my appearance, but I hadn't grown an inch since I graduated. No stature in my body, no stature among my peers at the school. Invisible again, naturally.

I didn't even attend the Saturday night shindig. Just spent the night with my parents and caught an early flight out the next morning. I'm sure nobody missed me.

I told myself at the time that I never wanted to relive that experience.

So why was I reconsidering now? I suppose I was just plain tired of being invisible. This could be my last chance to be…noticed. Admired even. I wasn't going to let that pass me by.

With less than eleven months until the reunion, I conceded that I was not going to be able to find a wife. My lack of success over the past fifty years was a track record too hard to ignore.

I needed a plan B.

I could go to Russia or China to "acquire" a wife. I had friends who'd had success in each country. Of course, their idea of success and mine were different, and I wasn't sure if a trophy wife was a top priority for either. I suspect one just wanted a maid. Okay, that was not going to work, this foreign escapade. Too many variables, and too little time to pull that off. And too much travel.

I could ask a friend to "pose" as my wife for the long weekend. That wasn't a stretch, but as I perused my female friends, I found none in the category of young, sexy, effervescent, funny, and affectionate. I didn't tend to attract that kind of woman, as I believe I made clear in excruciating detail. At least I had begun to define my edition of a trophy wife.

I could place an ad on one of the online dating sites. But as soon as I looked on one of the online dating sites, I immediately eliminated that option. Those things are scary—the sites, I mean, but of course, the women, too.

That left me with one option. I'd have to pay somebody to be my wife. I had money, so that might work.

As I began to jot down ideas, it felt like filling out a resume. Background and experience, strengths (not weaknesses), attributes (see above). I even went old school and added in height, weight, blond, shapely. Not very PC of me, but hey, if I'm making a wish list, might as well dream big, right?

Now that I had this outline sketch of my perfect woman, I needed to find her.

Where better to start than a talent agent? After all, I lived close to Los Angeles, and agents were plentiful. I found a firm that called themselves a talent agency and made an inquiring phone call. It did not go well.

The woman who answered the phone asked who I wanted to speak with.

"I'm looking to hire…a young…well, not real young…woman who could play my wife…for a weekend," I said.

"Which woman? We handle so many."

"I don't know."

"Is this for a movie or TV show?"

"Uh…neither?"

"Then do you mean like for a trade show? Somebody that could represent you? We handle several models."

"Uh…sure, that might work."

"Hold, please. I'll connect you," she said.

I waited longer than I expected—maybe she was explaining to the agent what I couldn't explain well to her.

Finally, I heard a male voice say, "This is Dominic. I hear you're looking for a model for a trade show. Is that right?"

"Well, no, not exactly," I replied.

"Then why don't you explain exactly what you're looking for, and we'll see if we can put something together."

Put something together? Like a Stepford Wife?

I let that thought pass and rambled on about my thoughts of a trophy wife for a long weekend at a high school reunion. As I began to read from my resume, he interrupted.

"Hold on, hold on. You're kidding me, right?"

"No, I'm serious."

"We don't do that kind of stuff, buddy. Get a life."

Then he hung up.

I didn't blame him. I had rambled quite a bit, and I only had a rough sketch of who and what I was looking for. But the assistant's comment—the one about "which woman"—gave me an idea.

I did some online research and found out that the agency I had contacted handled Hollywood talent. Actors and actresses.

Now we were getting somewhere. I just had to find the right *actress* to be my wife for the weekend. Why hadn't I thought of that before? It made perfect sense. A woman who could act like my wife, somebody who made a living posing as another person.

I eventually landed on one agency. I looked at their website and discovered all the talent they handled. I concentrated on the women, and even though I knew very few of the names, they were all striking. Then I began to notice stars who I recognized. Julianne Hough. Yes, I watched that dancing show. Sandra Bullock. Who doesn't know her? And she's what, like 50 years old? She would certainly qualify for a trophy wife no matter who was doing the judging.

Wait…who was I kidding? My idea suddenly began crashing down on me. Who was going to believe I was married to Sandra Bullock? Or any other famous actress.

I needed a Plan C. Or maybe just a Plan B 2.0, updated.

The next day I checked with some of the younger generation men that I worked with. I asked simple questions like: "If you saw some girl on TV or in the movies and you were really attracted to her, how would you find her? And if you did find her, how would you approach her?"

They told me to Google her. Really? It's that easy.

No, not so much I found out.

Late one night, I watched a Netflix movie about two women. Netflix has a whole catalog of movies with two women. Don't ask me how I know. Several had similar themes, like the one I was watching the night in question. The man in the movie done the one woman wrong and the other woman…sympathizes with her. And then…well…they get together. Nuff said.

The "you-done-me-wrong" woman struck me. Like upside the head with a love balloon. I rewound and watched it again from the time the two women fall in love. I gave away the plot, but you already figured it out so no harm.

She was perfect. The right age, shape, smile (oh, that smile!), perkiness, and everything. A brunette, but I hardly cared. Details, details. We could work it out.

Now, this is where it got interesting. I watched the credits, wrote both names down because I didn't know which woman was which—and wait for it—Googled them both. Voila! Found her.

Wikipedia told me more details, and who doesn't believe everything Wiki leaks to us. The detail I was most interested in—age—ticked off another box on my trophy wife resume. She was 39. That could work. It was a stretch, a big gap, but if I did a little of that Botox on my forehead…well, we're in the ballpark. Close enough for reunion work.

Because you might actually know her, I'll use a pseudonym, since we'd probably make up a name for her if she took the assignment. Let's call her Megan Starr. That's a fashionable first name, but not too exotic, for a woman of a certain age, like 39.

Now I dug deeper. I found out she was an actress and model, so from past painful experience, I knew I needed to find the agency that represented her. But I also had to change my tactic.

I doubled up on my Google searches and found the agency. I also ran across an article that explained many people had what is called an "assistant" who handled many of the details of their career. The agent handled the talent and bookings, but the assistant handled things like travel and clothes—logistical details like that.

Then I went back to the young men at my company with more questions. Okay, I found her, and who represents her, now how do I approach the assistant? Most told me to lie. Make up a whopper of a story. Like one, for instance, said to tell her I'd watched every movie she's ever been in, researched all the magazines in which she's appeared, and that I was head over heels in love. That should do it. Of course, most of these men didn't have serious relationships, so why was I listening to them?

I took another tack. I don't lie well. Most people don't, right? I know some people are full of it and some people lie through their enamels, but most people simply do a horrible job of telling lies.

So, I didn't. I decided to be myself. Mostly, I can pull that off. I wrote down my story and practiced it twenty-three times before I picked up the phone.

Alicia was the assistant. This is a synopsis of the phone conversation:

"Hi, this is Alicia."

"Hi, Alicia, my name is Ben. Do you work directly with Megan Starr?"

"I do, yes. How can I help you?"

"Well, this may sound a little weird, but here's my story. I saw Megan in this movie, *Two Forever*, and I thought she was…I mean is…just perfect for what I'm looking for. I need a date, let's call it, for my high school reunion. To show all those people that I can actually hang out with a fun, attractive, effervescent woman. You see, I never dated in high school. And most people…they didn't make fun of me or anything…most just ignored me. That made me extremely sad at the time, but I didn't know how to express it. Maybe I could hire Megan for a long weekend, pay all expenses, with absolutely no expectations, if you know what I mean. And we'd have fun together. Back in Pennsylvania. And I might add here that I think Megan is maybe the most attractive woman I have ever seen but never met. And maybe we could just meet and see if there is any possibility in the world that she would be interested in doing a…job, yes, it's a job…like this one."

I took a deep breath in the silence that followed. "Well, what do you think?"

"I think that's cute. Why don't you DM her?"

"Uh, DM?"

"Even cuter. DM means direct message. Like on Facebook. Tell her your story and see what happens. She's really nice, nicer than almost everyone I work with. She won't blow you off unless you go all creepy on her."

"I'm not a creep, really."

"I know, I know. Just suggest maybe a video chat after you exchange a few DMs or, if you're close to L.A., like a cup of coffee. Give it a shot. Who knows? Right?"

"Right. Thanks. I'll do that." I'd just have to figure out *how* to do that.

"And, Ben, if she doesn't respond right away, don't push too hard. She's really busy the next few weeks with a runway gig. If she doesn't answer, give me a call back, and I'll put in a good word for you, okay?"

"Thanks, Alicia. I really appreciate that."

"Absolutely. Good luck. Bye."

"Goodbye."

Plan B 2.0 on track and on target. But now what?

Long story short. I opened a Facebook page, asked how to get it started, populated it with a few clever—for me—posts, and the only two good photos of me where I don't look like a dork.

Then I punched in Megan Starr and found the one I was looking for of the sixteen listed.

Here was my first DM:

Hi, Miss Starr. I spoke with Alicia last week, and she recommended I contact you this way. Would it be okay with you if I sent another message outlining the job I have an opening for, which I think you'd be perfect for? It's a little out of the ordinary, more on the personal level, but nothing weird or creepy. Thanks, Ben

I waited a week and nothing. I checked my Facebook account several times a day. Okay, honestly, I checked every hour. Crickets. Nothing.

Just as I was about to call Alicia again, I saw a notice on my phone that I had a message.

Sure, fire away.

Contact! We have contact with Miss Starr! Now I had to figure out what to say next. I leaned toward the honesty route. It worked with Alicia; why not give it another try.

This may sound a little out of the box, but here's my story. I saw you in the movie, Two Forever, *and I thought you are just perfect for what I'm looking for. I need a date for my high school reunion. To show all those people that I can actually hang out with a fun, attractive, effervescent woman. I never dated in high school. Most people just ignored me. I became invisible. That made me extremely sad at the time, but I didn't know how to express it. If you're intrigued, I'd like to hire you as my date for a long weekend.*

Then I waited two more days before she replied.

I don't do that kind of work, sorry.

I didn't want to give up so quickly.

I can imagine. You must get a hundred requests like this every week. I'm not a young kid, starstruck with your beauty and doing this to impress my buddies. Actually, I'm kind of older, more mature. I'm not desperate. If you don't accept, I'll just not go. But it could be fun. What would make you reconsider?

Her reply came back within a minute.

Did you speak with my agent?

I tried, but he hung up on me. I did talk with Alicia.

Yeah, she mentioned she talked to you.

She didn't think I was creepy, did she?

No, she said you sounded, and I quote, adorable.

Full disclosure, I don't think anybody has ever called me that! Just want to be honest here.

Give me a week or two to think about it. What's the weekend?

Last weekend in July, the 26-29.

Bye for now.

Well, that went well, didn't it? I mean that was a conversation. Okay, I know it was digital, but hey, it's a start. As they say in my office, at least she didn't shoot me down completely. So, I waited.

As I went about my regular routines—work, I guess that is my only routine—my brain started to overreact. What if she had a husband? I didn't see one listed anywhere online that I could find. But maybe she had a boyfriend. Those things don't always show up, do they? I know many Hollywood couples like to flaunt their relationships. I guess that keeps them in the spotlight. But not all couples would be like that, would they?

What if she just flat out refused? Would I try to find another actress? I was beginning to fantasize about being with Megan and anybody else was not coming into the picture. I'd probably just not go, like I said to her in the message. But that was a bit depressing, too. I really did want to go, and I wanted to go with Megan, and I wanted to have all those people who always saw me as invisible see me with Megan Starr.

After eight days, twenty-one hours, and twelve minutes, I got a DM from Megan.

Where do you live?

West L.A., near Santa Monica.

I did an extensive background check on you.

How did it turn out? Anything I need to apologize for? I admit, I wore double knits in the '80s.

Funny. I was born in the '80s.

Ouch.

Maybe we could get together for a cup of coffee.

Definitely. When?

How about Thursday, 3 p.m.? You know the Bean There on Wilshire, your neighborhood?

Yes, I do. How will you recognize me?

Remember, background check. And double knits. C U then. Bye.

If I could do that dance that you see football players do, with one arm in front and one in back swinging, with hips swaying, I'd be doing that dance right now.

The next five days found me more nervous than I'd been in my life. Including the time I gave that speech in front of 350 engineers who didn't like what I had to say about their product.

I recognized her right away, sitting in the back of the coffee shop, in a baseball hat and sunglasses. Maybe actresses always dressed incognito.

"Hi, Miss Starr. I'm Ben," I said when she looked up. She took off the shades, smiled that smile, and I don't exactly remember what she said next.

We sat and enjoyed ourselves for fifteen minutes. Well, I enjoyed myself and she kept smiling, so I'm assuming she did, too. I noticed that even with her hair under the cap, it shone; it had a sparkle to it. I marveled at her skin. It was perfect. Not a blemish anywhere. Pink and fresh. To avoid staring directly at her, I looked at her hands and nails. Her fingers were long and slender, and her nails had a functional length with new polish. A light tangerine color I'd call it. They were perfect, too.

Then she started into the questions that I didn't particularly want to answer.

"So, why do you want to hire somebody to be your girlfriend for a weekend?"

"I knew you'd ask that," I began, "and I've been trying to come up with a decent answer where I don't look like a loser. But to be truthful, I suppose I want to impress those people."

"Why?" she asked, looking into my eyes and keeping contact until I looked away.

"I mean, it's been fifty years," she continued. "What do you care what they think?"

"I know I shouldn't, but I still do."

"Wouldn't they be impressed with everything you've accomplished? You've led a pretty full life. Have a good career. Even some peer recognition."

She wasn't kidding about the background check.

"But I've never been successful with women," I admitted. "And I don't want to go back alone. You've probably never felt that, being alone, I mean? You were probably a cheerleader in high school. And had a date every weekend. Lots of boyfriends...or sorry, maybe a steady one all the way through school. You probably never felt invisible. It's horrible." I didn't want to push her away or make her angry, but I needed to be honest.

She sat back in her chair and took another sip of her caramel soy latte and just looked at me. She didn't answer my questions, but she didn't have to.

"Can you afford my day rate?" she asked with a slight smile.

"What is it? I mean, yes, I can...I think," I answered, trying to sound confident and, I'm sure, failing.

"Fifteen hundred a day, not including expenses."

"Do you charge the same rate for travel days?"

Her smile broadened with that one. "What do you mean?"

"Well, when I hire myself out, I only charge my half-day rate if I'm traveling the whole day and not working. And on this trip, there would be two full days of just travel since it's back East."

"We might be able to negotiate something there," she said.

Now I was the one smiling. We sat smiling at each other.

"Now what?" I asked.

"If we're going to do this, and I'm not saying I'm fully committed yet, I have a few ideas."

"Okay, like what?"

"First, no offense, but we work on your wardrobe a bit. Do you mind?"

I shook my head.

"And maybe a nice new haircut, and...something about that beard. I don't know what yet."

I shrugged. No big deal.

"How long are you going to tell your friends that we've been dating?" she asked with another sip.

"Hadn't thought of that. I guess long enough that it would seem like a serious relationship but not so long as they'd wonder why we weren't married...or living together."

"Let's settle on nine months. That's when relationships get serious. You're past the initial drinks-and-dinner phase, and you're beginning to evaluate something long-term. Work for you?" She leaned closer to me and propped her hand under her chin.

"Sure."

"So, if we've been dating for that long, we're going to have to get to know one another well enough to pull that off. You know, we don't want to get caught off guard. We have to be able to answer the simple stuff, like how we met, what we like to do together, favorite restaurants, where we like to vacation together. Things like that."

"And how do we do that?" I thought I knew the answer, but it would be good hearing her say it. It seemed to me that she was talking herself into this job. I wiped at imaginary crumbs on the table.

"We set up a couple of sessions."

Sessions didn't sound like what I was thinking. I didn't actually *know* what I was thinking, but sessions reminded me of therapy.

"One at your place, and one at mine. So, we get to know each other. You write down all the pertinent questions you think they'll ask, and we'll come up with the scenario together."

This sounded more like an assignment.

"We'll do kind of a script. I can follow a script. That's what I do." Again, that smile spread across her face.

I smiled back because I knew for sure I'd like the assignment.

The first session happened at her home. She owned a small but stylish house in the Brentwood area of L.A. I guess it was about 1,500 square feet, but every inch was immaculate. I made a mental note to have my place professionally cleaned when the session work moved to my home.

"I think we need to start out by coming up with five things we like to do together," she began. "So, I like to run on the beach."

"I'll watch you from one of those abandoned lifeguard shacks. To make sure nobody harasses you," I countered. "'Cause I don't run, on the beach or…anywhere."

"I like the detail, good. Next, I like to eat in fancy restaurants."

"I like to eat, too."

"Okay, two for two. I like to go to Europe for vacations."

"I'm good with that as long as there are no beaches to run on and lots of restaurants to try."

She flashed me that smile, and I felt like we connected. At least I hoped so.

"I like to attend Broadway plays in New York," she added.

"Never been there," I confessed.

Her eyes grew wide, and she tried to mask her horror at the admission and quickly morphed it into a smile. I settled for that.

"Hey, I should have asked you this before we started. Are you charging me your daily rate for today?" I asked with a little humor in my voice.

"Hmm, good question. It is Saturday, and I usually don't work on Saturday. Maybe I'll cut you a break."

"How about I take you out to a fancy restaurant after the session? As payment?"

"Deal," she said. Then we ironed out a few more details of our fake relationship.

We met several times over the next month, at her place and mine and a few fancy restaurants. But we still had four months until the reunion, and I began to wonder how I could extend the session work between now and then. She didn't seem to think we knew each other well enough (at least that's what I assumed), and I wasn't going to broach the subject. A few times, I actually didn't think of it as session work and began to fantasize that we were on a real date. I met a few of her friends in a bar one night when we were waiting for a table at a fancy restaurant in Venice Beach. I invited her—boldly, I might add on my part—to a birthday party of one of my friends.

Then she began to travel extensively in the spring for her work. She didn't call or text or make any attempt to contact me at all while she was gone. I tried not to feel hurt. Didn't work.

When she returned, I visited her hair stylist, got a mani/pedi, and had my beard professionally trimmed. We spent a day shopping for a few new outfits for me and two for her. I paid for them all.

A week before we were to fly to Pennsylvania for the reunion, we met in a fancy restaurant in Santa Monica to "review the script," as she put it.

"Okay, are we ready for this?" she began.

"I think so. We've got how we met, what we like to do, where you were born and raised, how you got into the business, and you know enough about my work to fake it pretty well."

"Yeah, if I knew more, they'd know I was too well rehearsed. I can always play the dumb starlet if they ask too many questions about Boboli."

"Boboli? That's a pizza crust. Do you mean Boolean, like the computer logic we talked about?"

She radiated, and I couldn't tell if she was serious or not.

"You've got the tickets, right?" she asked.

"Yes, and I rented a nice SUV."

"Where are we staying?"

"The nicest hotel in town…and that ain't saying much."

She raised her eyebrows and cocked her head to the right with a little silent *ooh* on her lips but said nothing.

"I think we forgot one thing. And it may kill the whole deal, blow our cover sky-high," I said.

"Oh, what's that?"

"We have to kiss. I mean, we can't do a fake kiss in front of everyone and pull that off. You know, like in that movie with Sandra Bullock and Ryan what's-his-name? A dead giveaway," I said, now really getting bold.

"*The Proposal* was the film. I fake-kiss in the movies all the time. That's not a problem for me."

"But I don't." Where was this bold me coming from? "I probably need the practice."

She tapped her forefinger on the table, making me wait out

her decision. I didn't pull back the request.

I leaned closer and gave her a quick—way too quick—kiss on her lips, barely brushing them.

"No pass, dead giveaway," she said. "Come here."

I complied as requested.

"Now, that's a Hollywood kiss," she said.

It certainly was.

Early Thursday morning of reunion week, we shared an Uber to LAX. It dropped us off at United, and we made our way inside and lined up at the counter. We checked our bags, and the attendant told us the gate number was 70, pointing to the security line on the floor above.

As we waited in line, Megan looked at the overhead screen to check the gate number.

"I think she got the gate wrong. That plane goes to Kennedy in New York. We're headed to Pittsburgh."

I shook my head. "Nope."

"What do you mean, nope?"

"We're headed to Broadway and all the fancy restaurants I can afford in New York City."

"What about the reunion?" she said, smiling that smile.

"That was when I felt invisible."

She grabbed my hand, leaned in, and kissed me. It sure didn't feel like a Hollywood kiss this time.

Dialogue Duplex

Woman

I just need some comfort food. I'm not really hungry, just feeling a little empty. I don't even know where that empty feeling comes from. What do I have to feel empty about?

It's past lunchtime, but I know this little place serves all day. I like it here. Warm and comfortable, cocoonish. Friendly, but not overly. I don't need friends right now, just some food. Maybe a little pasta. Oh, the minestrone soup! That should fill me up.

But I'm not hungry.

Man

I just need a drink. Jeez, it's early for a drink. Why am I craving a drink? Should I be worried about that? Well, maybe just one. I'm feeling on edge. But wait…on the edge of what? What does *on edge* even mean?

Dang, it's two o'clock. But that little place has a restaurant, so it's not just a bar. I couldn't go into a bar at two o'clock in the afternoon. And I'll only have a beer or a glass of burgundy, nothing hard.

It's two o'clock in the afternoon.

Woman

I'm feeling a little down. Down from what? Sometimes I feel up, I guess, but it seems like I feel down way more than up.

What do I have to feel down about? Nothing I can think of. No big gaps in my life. But there could be more. More what? I guess what I mean is, *I* could be more. My job is fun but not fulfilling at all. Doing more. But how do I do that? My day is full, but I do waste a lot of time, mostly in front of the TV. Every time I try to add significance into my life, it falls a little short. Can I really do it? Produce more in my career or find a fulfilling job? Is it even in me? Am I up to it? I don't know.

Oh, sure, I'm ready to order. I'll have a big bowl of the minestrone. And maybe a side salad. With chicken. A little extra dressing on the side.

I probably won't eat it all.

Man

I feel like crap. Just one of those days, I guess. I'll kill it tomorrow. Hopefully. Man, these kinds of days are just piling up on me here. Where is all that coming from?

Where the heck am I? I'm not where I should be, that's for sure. I should be more, achieving more. Bigger bucks. Bigger job. Bigger... something.

Yeah, well, how's that working out? C'mon, suck it up. What are you, a wimp?

Bourbon, rocks. With a splash.

I'm gonna have just one.

Woman

Okay, I don't have a man right now, but so what? I've been down that road, man-less avenue, and it's worked out just fine. I could probably find a man—if I really wanted one. I could still do that. I'm not such a bad catch.

That might be nice again.

We could do things. Be together. Plan a trip. Or a weekend. Or longer.

That *would* be nice.

A man.

Man

I'm a little lonely. Horny, too. I haven't been lonely since Gloria left. Whew, Gloria. I could think about that woman all day long.

And Rachel. Um, um…Rachel. Why did we ever break up? I wish Rachel was sitting right next to me now.

Or Gloria.

No, Rachel. Definitely Rachel.

Woman

Take a couple of deep breaths. Two more. Feel better. C'mon.

Man

Maybe I need to work out tonight. How long's it been? Maybe pump a little iron.

Woman

Was he looking at me? Why would he be looking at me? All I wanted was a nice little lunch in a nice, cozy place. Just time alone, by myself, no distractions.

He *wasn't* looking at me. Was he? He couldn't be. Not me.

He'd better turn back around.

Don't look his way. Two more deep breaths.

Man

Who is that? Hot mama.

Nice bod. I wish I could see more. I wonder where she came from. How did I miss that? I must be slipping.

Huh. She looks a little like Gloria. Only probably taller. And maybe, what, ten or twenty pounds heavier? She's probably a little older. Harder to keep the weight off when you hit that age. I like her dress, classy. Can't see her legs though, and I'm a leg man.

Was I staring? Oh, well, what could it hurt?

Gloria.

Woman

Maybe he *was* looking at me. Should I flirt a little? Just to see what happens? What's the worst that could happen? Ew. I don't even want to go there.

Why's he keep looking at me? What, he thinks he's God's gift to women or something? They're all alike.

I'm not gonna flirt with someone like him. No way, Jose.

Oh, goodness, why did I just smile at him? What's wrong with me? I can't even control myself. Now he'll think I'm into all this. Look away, look away. Don't look at him.

Man

Did she just smile at me? Oh, baby, yeah. Like taking candy from a … that was a smile, wasn't it?

Now what do I do? Walk over, say hello? That's kinda cheesy. Send a drink over? A drink of what? She's not even drinking. Slip the bartender a note? What, am I in high school?

Suck it up, suck it up. What's the next move here? C'mon, think, think.

Woman

Do not smile. Do not smile. Control yourself. Stay calm. Act nonchalant. Deep breath. You are not what he thinks you are.

Jerk.

Man

Stay cool. Stay cool. But be a little aggressive. Women like that. Smile again. Maybe a nod of the head to say you see her, you notice her, you like what you see.

Oh, baby.

Woman

I've had just about enough of this guy. I know he's looking at me again. I can feel it. Beady little eyes all over me.

What? Oh, I'm sorry. No, nothing more, thanks. Wait, wait. I think I'll order something. Hmm, let's see. How about a bowl of pasta with spaghetti sauce?

What? No, a full order. Yes, for here.

Man

I sure would like to get to know this chick. I can tell she's avoiding me, playing hard to get. No eye contact, but that smile. Sweet. No games here, baby girl, 'cause what you see is what you get.
Yep, you still got it. Uh-huh. Uh-huh.
Yeah, sure. I'll have another, hit me again. Make it a Jack this time.

Woman

Yes, thanks, it was delicious. I left a little extra here in the tip. That's for cleanup and in case the bowl breaks or something. You'll see. Sorry in advance. But a lesson needs to be taught here. I hope you'll understand.
Courage, courage. Deep breath. Let it out slowly.

Man

She's leaving? With a bowl of pasta in her hand?

Woman

See head, deposit pasta!

Man

What! Are you kidding me! Stay cool. Stay cool. Don't give her the satisfaction of a reaction.

Woman

Ta-dah!!

Man

I'm pretty sure I didn't order that.

Woman

Oh, you did, that's for sure. And I just delivered it.

Don't Guess Who's Coming to Dinner

"**H**ow was your day, hon?" my wife asked when I walked in the door.

Distracted, as usual these days, I said, "Fine, nothing earth-shattering."

"Oh, I'm glad for that." She smiled her usual smile. "Want a little chardonnay?"

I nodded, grabbed a wine glass from the cupboard, and she tipped a generous pour. I leafed through the pile of mail that she rarely retrieved from the mailbox and almost never sorted. I tossed a few catalogs and other junk mail.

"Let me see those," she said.

I shook my head as I retrieved the catalogs from the recycling bin. I knew she would never read them, and they'd collect dust for the next week on the hutch. And then I'd throw them away anyway, so why bother to keep them? I rolled my eyes for emphasis, which she ignored out of courtesy, and, I suppose, love. Okay, yes, I know, she loves me. But it often seems we're inundated with catalogs.

"I'm going to go change my clothes," I muttered, heading upstairs.

"Oh, I almost forgot. Benji is coming to dinner," she said. "And he's bringing a young lady."

I stopped on the second stair. "Our son is bringing a girl to dinner? Must be serious."

"I have no idea, but Derek, don't ask him while she's here.

He said it's only their second date, so go easy on him."

"Maybe I can corner him when she's out of earshot."

He probably won't say a thing and tell me sarcastically that's really not something I need to know.

Just before seven, the doorbell rang, and being the closest, I lumbered over to open it. I wondered what the young lady looked like. My son usually brought home very cute, bubbly women.

I opened the door and froze. Just stared, unable to move.

"Uh, hi, Dad," my son said, trying to break through.

Oh my, it's her!

I did my best *sorry* look and said, "Oh, sorry. Hi, hi, come on in. I'm Derek, the dad." I extended my hand. She shook it, and she leaned in to give me an almost hug.

"Hi, I'm Angelina."

She smelled heavenly. I recognized her immediately. I'd seen that face a hundred times and always wondered what her name might be. Angelina.

Angel.

"Come in, come in, come in," I stuttered.

They came in, she met my wife, Ann, and we poured more wine. My son declined; he had a race the next day and always refrained from alcohol for forty-eight hours before he ran.

During the pre-meal banter in the kitchen, I caught Angelina staring at me with a quizzical look on her face.

Uh-oh.

"You look so familiar to me. Do I know you from someplace?" she asked without conviction.

She remembered me. She knew me all right, and she knew that she knew me. I felt mortified.

"Yeah, you look familiar, too," I said with as much nonchalance as I could muster.

"I'll figure it out." She smiled back without the same sincerity I'd noticed in her smile before.

Oh, terrific.

During dinner, as the conversation sagged, I asked my son, "So, Benj, you've got a race tomorrow?"

"Yeah, it's just a 10K. Down at the beach and not much elevation. I'm not really in race shape, but I'm pretty sure I can finish in the top twenty, maybe even crack the top ten in my age group."

"Are you running, too?" Ann asked Angelina.

"Oh, no, I'm not a runner. More like a gym rat."

Rat would not be the word I'd use for her—in any matter of conversation.

"With my studies, I don't really have time to train much and running just seems so…repetitive." She chuckled, lightly punching my son in the arm.

He smiled back at her.

"What are you studying?" Ann asked again, since I was in some sort of fog, not quite a fantasyland but not present and accounted for.

"I'm just finishing my second year of nursing."

Oh my, she's a college student.

"I hope to go into pediatric care, maybe with kids with cancer and other serious problems," she continued, "but it'll take a bit of work to get there."

"It sounds so noble," Ann noted. "And a little depressing, to tell the truth."

She's noble, too.

Angelina pondered that without comment, slightly nodding her head, not in agreement, just in thought.

"Well, Dad, how's your workout plan coming along?" Benji interjected, to break the previous conversation.

I really, really didn't like the direction of this question, so I threw up my standard shield. "Still trying to lose those ten pounds. More wine, anyone?"

"Oh, do you work out, Derek?" Angelina asked.

Really, really.

I pinched my thumb and forefinger together, indicating a

little.

"Don't be so modest, hon," Ann said, "You're at the Y five days a week." She smiled that smile again.

I looked at the girl, and she frowned. Then her eyes grew big. Like she had discovered something.

Like me.

"You work out at the Y," she said as a statement, not a question.

"Bingo. Mystery solved," my son said.

Angelina just nodded, without a smile at all.

Bingo, I'm dead.

"Is that how you know my husband, Angelina?" Ann again.

My wife, the prober.

"Yeah, that could be it. I'll have some more wine, please," she countered, offering up a half full glass.

The rest of the dinner went by in a blur. Angelina seemed distracted, answering most questions quickly, without detail.

After dessert, she blurted out, "I really should be going." And leaning toward Benji, "I'll Uber home. I've got a couple of stops, and I know you need your rest for the race tomorrow."

She pushed her chair back, grabbed her phone, and began to walk to the door.

"Hey, hold on." Benji raised his voice. "What just happened?"

"Let me talk to her," I said out of somewhere.

"What?" he asked.

"Just let me try," as I headed to the door. Ann look confused, Benji startled.

She had made it to the porch and cradled her phone in her hand, summoning Uber, I guess.

"Angelina, wait a minute."

"No, no, everything's fine. I just need to leave now."

"I think we need to talk. Right?"

She just stared at me, then quickly looked away, shaking her head. She repeatedly stabbed at the phone with her forefinger.

"Do I have something I need to apologize for?" I asked.

Her eyes just grew huge, as if to say, *You're kidding me, right?* She blinked twice for emphasis.

Why did I even ask? I knew the answer.

I paced around the porch. Benji stuck his head out the door, and I waved him away. He closed the door but left it open a crack. I grabbed the handle and pulled it shut.

Angelina looked back at me, cocked her head, and looked like she was waiting for an explanation.

"I've seen you at the gym."

Her face darkened, eyes squinty.

"I think you're very…attractive, no…cute, you know."

Eyes bulging again. Finger punching phone.

"I'm sorry if I did something inappropriate," I whispered.

She looked into my eyes with a combination of determination and hurt. "I saw the way you looked at me. Not cool. At all."

I cringed, and I'm sure it showed on my face. I shrunk away with humiliation.

"I didn't realize…I'm sorry," I managed. But, of course, I did realize. I was weak around young women, trying not to look and failing most times. I didn't leer, did I? I just looked, right? Looking's not so bad, but leering…I know, that's bad. I'd crossed the line with Angelina—from looking to leering. Thank God, I hadn't made a pass at her.

As the Uber pulled up and she got in the car, she said, "Tell Benji goodbye," with a wave of her hand, as if she was swatting a fly away. She never looked back.

I had nothing to say, nowhere to go.

The front door opened again, and Benji and Ann stood there with confused expressions, waiting for some explanation.

What could I say? I ogled your girlfriend?

I did my best to wipe what I knew was guilt from my face.

"I don't know what just happened," I said, my two hands up in surrender.

I could tell by the looks on their faces that they didn't believe it.

I could try, "That's not really something you need to know," but that would sink me deeper.

"I offended her in some way, I guess," I confessed.

That really wasn't much of a confession I knew. But how could I confess to more?

Stone silence from the two of them.

Benji looked disgusted and walked away. Ann held one hand to her mouth, gasped an audible breath, and walked away.

None of us ever saw Angelina again.

Death by a Thousand Little Touches

"Where are you going?" I asked, thinking I heard Joe wrong.

"Chicago," he mumbled again.

"Why are you going there?"

"To see Jeannie."

"My Jeannie?" My voice was louder than I expected.

"You said you were done with her, Davey. That you were back with your wife," Joe said, a little defiance creeping into his comeback.

He was right, that was what I'd said, and I wanted to mean it. With all my heart—well, most of it—I wanted to be over Jeannie. But I wasn't. I could tell that immediately. "She invited you?"

He nodded, not meeting my stare.

For the past month, I'd confided in Joe, late at night after we finished cleaning up the kitchen in the small apartment we shared. He'd been my roommate for three months. After my wife asked me to leave our home, Jeannie had visited that apartment often. Joe knew her, knew how pretty she was, and knew how I felt about her. He knew I loved her, but Joe also knew I was trying to love my wife and family more.

"What's the purpose of your visit?" I blurted out in a formal tone. I didn't want to hear the answer.

He looked at me like I couldn't be serious. "She's lonely. That's all."

Typical Jeannie. She'd used that complaint so often I'd

become immune to her need. But not Joe. We're all lonely, most of the time, aren't we? Even if we're married, we can be lonely. It's a terrible feeling, like you're the last person on Earth who deserves love. Jeannie's exact words. I always wanted to soothe her and tell her, no, you are worthy of love. Then I'd love her, for a while. She was okay with it until I left, and then she'll call or text and tell me how lonely she was, and I'd fall back into trying to make her feel less lonely. Man, we just went round and round that old tale.

But when Joe said she was lonely, my heart felt the tug, the ache. I wanted to rush to her again because not only would I help her, but I'd be the one who would save her from loneliness. I'd be the hero. I'd feel good—and needed. We all need to feel needed, don't we?

I sulked off to my room and shut the door, reaching for my headphones and tuning into a little Neil Young music. Something about the hard rock and whining vocals of Young brewed sadness in me.

I'd met Jeannie at a trade show. My company had me scouting small firms to acquire, and the firm she was working for made a complementary product to our line. When I approached the booth, her smile hit me like a punch to the stomach—completely took my breath away. She sparkled in that bright blue suit, showing off her slender figure perfectly. She'd laugh, and her smile spread over her entire body as she engaged with people, touching them on the forearm or hand for emphasis. Jeannie had a booth full of customers so we couldn't talk long. I took the first misstep.

I asked her to dinner and got to know her that night over Italian food at a quiet little restaurant tucked away in a Chicago neighborhood. We lingered, first talking about business, then the life of traveling salespeople. Finally, she asked the question I didn't want to answer.

"So, are you married?"

I waited a few beats too long before managing, "I am."

"Children?"

I nodded, "We just had our second. He's four months old."

She smiled but not so much to me as to herself. I still remember that smile.

I'd already failed to notice my next little missteps. Looking back, I didn't notice much of anything about the beginning of our romance.

By the third trip to Chicago, I'd leave on a Friday to spend the weekend and miss church on Sunday, often times not returning until Tuesday or Wednesday. I always told my wife it was business, and I suppose she believed me at first.

I hadn't fallen out of love with my wife, Beth. But when we started having children, something changed. With just the two of us, we could get all our needs met. We could please the other person and get satisfaction almost simultaneously. Not just sexually. I mean in most all aspects of life. I didn't just want to make myself happy. Well, I mean, I did, of course. But I also wanted to make sure my wife was happy. I didn't always put her first—does any husband do that all the time? But I didn't demand that she make me happy; I didn't insist that she care for me more than for herself. I wasn't that bad. We're all self-centered to a point, right?

When we had kids, I lost part of her. I wasn't jealous of my children for taking her away from me, but I felt less important to her. I couldn't contribute to her like I had. I couldn't make her happy—that seemed to be what the kids did. I struggled with my reduced role.

She was wrapped up with a three-year-old and a newborn. I hired her part-time help, a high-school girl from our church who would come in after school and a few hours on weekends to help with the kids and cleaning and cooking. That gave me a little freedom and a sense that I was helping, when, in fact, I mostly felt useless around the house. We'd almost given up keeping the home in order, the way I liked it. I could change my son's diapers, but that was all I was entrusted with. Even when I took care of our daughter, my wife often criticized my time with our toddler. In a nice way—she didn't come down hard on me. She's never like that. I admit, it was hard relating to little girls. I grew up in a family of boys with three brothers. When I tried to wrestle on the floor with my little girl like all my buddies did with their little boys, she shrieked like I was hurting her—I wasn't—and ran to her mom.

My wife told me boys liked to wrestle but girls liked to play make-believe.

So, I found a girl that liked to play that way. Her name was Jeannie.

At first, the spurts of time I spent in Chicago filled me with new adventures. Jeannie had a condo near the Loop downtown. We spent late nights checking out the bar scene. We strolled around Millennium Park, taking in local theater and ice skating. She surprised me one Saturday with tickets in the left field bleachers at a Cubs game. New sights to see, new restaurants, a new woman who adored me. And incredible sex. I hadn't made love to my wife since the baby was born. We tried once, and when I finally got her naked in bed, the baby wailed from the nearby crib and milk gushed from her breasts like a broken sprinkler. She shoved me off and went to feed our son.

That everything-new feeling with Jeannie lasted four or five months.

By this time, my wife knew that I had been unfaithful. The phone calls, the texts, the unexplained business trips, and my lack of enthusiasm for our marriage led her to confront me. I loved my wife enough to confess—at least, I told myself that. Hard to figure now how that thinking crept into me—that I confess my infidelity to somehow confirm my love for her. Man, what was I thinking?

One night after we got the kids to bed, we opened a bottle of merlot and I confessed. Everything. Well, almost everything.

I told Beth that I had to figure out if Jeannie was the woman I wanted to spend the remainder of my life with. I emphatically conveyed that I still loved her but that Jeannie somehow needed me more now in her life. That I believed I was contributing to Jeannie's life in a way that I couldn't—or didn't want to—for my family. I'm sure that sounded to my wife like lunacy or betrayal or abandonment. Or all three. I didn't quite understand it myself.

My wife asked me to move out, and that's when Joe and I found that two-bedroom apartment. Jeannie visited every other month or so in between my trips to Chicago, and the more time I spent with her, the less she seemed to need me. She started to criticize little things I did that made no sense to me. Like eating my steak rare or failing miserably at suppressing a burp. Beth always had the ability to convey her lack of enthusiasm for badly timed man behaviors with a sly smile and head tilt.

With Jeannie, small disagreements blew up into big arguments. She sulked if I held my ground when we quarreled. And I was lonely for my wife and kids.

Joe left for Chicago that weekend, and I called my wife and invited her to lunch. I hadn't seen her in two months. Miraculously, she accepted. I'd forgotten how gracious she could be. The kids came, too, and the reunion was loving and boisterous. The kids took turns sitting in my lap. My daughter showed me her doll, and we held a three-way conversation. When I looked into her eyes, I noticed they were the exact same color as my wife's, pale blue. My son kept looking up at me and stroking my beard with one hand and banging a spoon on the table with the other. I kissed his head, and the smell of baby shampoo lingered. It looked to me like the slight curl in his hair would soon morph into the messy mop of tangles in my own.

But all the commotion made it so difficult to talk with my wife that I felt incomplete when we parted, even though we made arrangements to get together for dinner in another few days. I missed my kids, and I missed companionship with my wife—from little things like sharing my day to bigger conversations like planning the future. I'd forgotten how well my wife listened to me and understood both my frustrations in life and how I often failed to understand how to deal with my feelings. She knew me so well she could be honest with me—tough, even—without being critical or judgmental. Beth cherished being able to help me that way, and I loved that her patience with me seemed to be almost endless. Until now. How could I have forgotten all that so quickly?

Later, in the throes of more sad music, I realized that I missed being needed almost as much as I missed them. That confused me. I thought marriage would be a mutual relationship where both parties relied and depended on each other equally. But now, my wife needed me less, and I needed that satisfaction of being loved more. Of course, I didn't fully realize what was taking place as it happened.

Beth took the kids back East to visit her parents. When Joe returned from Chicago, I avoided any talk of his time with Jeannie. Until she called me.

"I miss you," she said before hello.

It felt like a knife slicing open a chamber of my heart.

"I thought you had company this weekend," I said, trying to keep my voice controlled.

"He isn't you. No one is you. You're the one I need. And I'm the one that you need. Don't you know that by now?"

"I'm not sure."

"I think you are, but you don't want to admit it."

"I'm trying to make it work with my wife," I blurted.

Silence.

Then, in almost a whisper, "It hasn't worked so far. Why do you think it will ever work?"

I wanted to shout, because it's supposed to, and it had for the first five years. Because the heavens above ordained it, or because I couldn't comprehend a divorce. But my silence only gave her strength.

"Come to me, Davey," she said.

"What?"

"I need you. Now. Meet me in Cabo next week."

After she hung up, I searched for flights.

The first few days in Mexico disappointed me. I thought it would be bliss. But it was ever-so-slightly off, like a wheel out of balance. We drank and ate and played in the surf, but after a week, I observed small demands coming from our talks that I hadn't noticed before.

My wife had never wanted to vacation in exotic places, saying that we needed to save for our children's education. I agreed—and we did take short trips in state—but I often felt like life was laborious, lacking fun or excitement. Time with Jeannie was always fun, except when I started to hear those demands.

"Now that your wife has left you for her parents…" she began one night, her eyes piercing into mine. We were sitting in one of our favorite Cabo bars. Tiki torches illuminated the perimeter, and soft lights strung along an overhead trellis cast shadows on our table. We'd kicked off our sandals and dug our toes into the cool, white sand.

"She's just visiting. She hasn't left," I replied without much conviction.

"What makes you think they will allow her to return?"

"What do you mean?"

"She is their daughter, and you are the villain. You cheated on her, and they will never forgive you for that." A single nod of her head acted like a judge's gavel slamming down to end the discussion.

"You don't know that to be true," I said through clenched teeth. But I wasn't sure either.

"Oh, believe me, it's true. And it will be a really short leap of faith, as you like to put it, to the time when they will want to support her and the children and eliminate you from their life entirely. It's coming. It won't be hard to poison your wife and kids to that reality."

I hadn't thought of that. The waiter walked past a table away, and I motioned for another round. The tropical breeze blew the acrid smell of kerosene from the torches toward us, and I tasted the fumes.

"So, you'd better make plans to save some of your money. And to begin to think of your life after they cut you out of your family's life completely. You deserve to be happy, don't you?"

She didn't add the "with me" at the end of the sentence. Was I imagining that? Could I accept that?

As the waiter delivered a third round of drinks and we nibbled on the crab legs appetizer, I began to envision a life beyond my marriage. I kept asking myself: Is there more to life than this? Will I ever feel that way again—the way I felt when I first fell in love with my wife? Could it be possible with Jeannie? Maybe it was the crab, but my stomach felt queasy.

As our bodies tanned and absorbed more food and alcohol over the next week, Jeannie became testy. Even belligerent.

She began to lash out at me—about the way I cooked salmon (too dry) and the way I let my beard grow (too gross). Little things, really, nothing substantial. And all were unexpected. It had been almost great for a while and now…almost horrible.

When I told her the next day that I was planning to leave, she shrugged and asked me to buy her return flight to Chicago. I did.

Again, my emotions flooded with confusion—with sadness and regret mixed in. She had told me repeatedly that she was miserable without me. Now, it seemed she was just as miserable with me.

Once I was home, I couldn't understand why Beth and kids weren't back from her parents yet. Even though we hadn't spoken in weeks, she'd told me before they left that it was going to be just a short visit. When I called her, she confirmed Jeannie's suspicions. Almost.

"It's been so comfortable here. Mom helps with the kids, and Dad does much of the cooking. I think the kids are really enjoying being around their grandparents."

"I see," I said.

"The kids miss you, Davey. I miss…." I could hear her gulping for her next breath.

That surprised me and caught me off guard. I blurted, "Oh, Beth, I'm such an idiot. I don't even know what I want anymore.'

It sounded lame and incomplete, and she knew immediately what I meant.

"You are such an..." But I didn't hear the rest because she had hung up.

Over the past several months even before my wife and I separated, I'd been meeting with two guys from church early each Wednesday morning before work. It wasn't an official Bible study or an accountability group, just guys hanging out. I'd kept my secret from them, but I felt dishonorable because of it.

One week after Cabo, I confessed. Everything. They both had anger in their eyes, but surprisingly, they forgave me. But they both urged me, almost demanded, that I give up Jeannie and do whatever I could to win back my wife. I knew in my heart that was what I wanted. It was my only choice, they said. Unfortunately, they were wrong.

I forged ahead to try and save my marriage. I apologized. I begged. I pleaded. I wrote a heartfelt letter to her parents. I even spent an evening with her older sister and told her how despicable I had become. She agreed with me and said, beyond the earshot of my wife, that if it were her, I'd be history faster than that car in "Back to the Future," but that she wouldn't influence her sister.

Good luck and I hope you make it and I'll even pray for you as much as I don't want to, but I really, really doubt that you make it because, as you said so yourself, you're despicable.

Throughout the separation, my wife and I talked on the phone every other week, mostly about money. Trying to sustain two households put a severe strain on our cash flow. We'd met in person once in a coffee shop so we could review the checkbook and bank statement. I'd forgotten how calm and organized she could be in the midst of chaos. That's not my strong suit. She mentioned her folks had given her several thousand dollars to help with essentials, and I immediately felt frustrated that I'd let the family down. Again. This time financially. Eventually, we started to meet at our home so we could balance the checkbook—and I could see the kids.

I asked her if she'd be willing to see a marriage counselor. At first, she was reluctant, but I persisted, and we began the process. In therapy, I confessed and begged for forgiveness. When the counselor met with both of us—we had individual sessions, too—Beth was sullen and reluctant to accept my apology. I couldn't blame her. When we were asked to give three examples of things we loved about our spouse, I quickly replied, but Beth struggled to find anything.

My wife and I began spending one evening a week together after work. We'd make dinner, bathe the kids, read them to sleep, and spend another hour or so talking. Even though I wanted to spend the night, I always left and returned to a new apartment I'd found closer to my house. And farther away from Joe.

I refused to acknowledge the text messages I got almost daily from Jeannie. When she called, I never picked up and never returned the messages. And they became even nastier the longer I neglected her. They had started out sad, pleading with me to contact her. How miserable she was without me. Same old, same old. But gradually her messages became threatening. Nothing specific, just that I didn't know what she was capable of and not to underestimate her and how I really didn't want to reject her.

One night after two beers of supplemental strength, I called Jeannie back.

"I'm back with my wife," I began, and although it wasn't technically true, I knew in my heart I wanted it to be.

"It won't work. I told you that," she replied without emotion.

"It seems to be now."

"You don't want this. She doesn't take care of you. You need someone to take care of you. I do that."

I faltered for a second and thought about that. She might be right. But I found a tiny bit of strength to battle. "I don't think you're right," I managed.

That was the proverbial straw. "Then you're nothing to me," she said and ended the call.

I breathed deep and thanked God, repeatedly. I felt renewed, not quite born again because I knew how dirty I'd become, but I had hope, at last.

That feeling lasted six hours.

Jeannie struck back with a vengeance. Somehow, she had obtained an email list of mine. I never knew how she got it. But when I read the email that she sent to all—and I mean every single one of my friends in my digital address book—I swear I didn't breathe for five minutes. My heart stopped beating.

It outlined almost every transgression I had committed with her. The sex, the lies—thank heavens there wasn't a videotape. She posted several photos of us kissing and hugging, too. Everything. To everyone.

Five minutes later, I saw another email land like a bomb in my inbox. The same letter with a few additions addressed to my in-laws and my parents. *What, did you hack into my address book on my phone?* My parents just read that. My in-laws just read that. I almost cried.

Then, later that evening—I checked every minute or so—the final hand grenade. A new letter, with almost all of the details of the previous ones, addressed to—good God, no—my wife. She included a tidy little section in the email with screen captures of my many text messages to her. Intimate messages.

Affairs in the digital world—death by a thousand little touches.

I was mortified. I was embarrassed. Livid. Suicidal. Crushed. Defeated. Dead.

Immediately, all communication to and from my wife and her parents was severed. A few friends sent condolence messages disguised as "how in the world could you have been with a woman like that?" questions hanging in the air. My mom reached out to me, but I found it so hard to talk to her that I didn't return her call. I only sent a voicemail message when I knew she wouldn't pick up, apologizing and telling her I couldn't even form words right now. I'd call soon. My dad, never much for talk, sent a text that I kept.

It read: *My God. She-devil.*

I began to sense the humiliation I knew must be crushing my wife. Everything I'd achieved in life as a husband and father was lost by what my wife was going through. I knew what my friends and family were thinking and saying about me—how dishonorable I'd become—but I could survive that. I didn't know if the humiliation and mortification I realized my wife had to endure would ever heal. That devastated me more than anything.

I battled this inferno for four months. When Christmas arrived, I reached out to my wife. She texted back that I was forbidden to spend time with the family. Her parents were in town, and they wanted nothing to do with me, EVER. She capitalized that word in the text.

But she would meet me at a coffee shop on Christmas Eve, if I wanted. It was a flicker, and I grabbed at the light.

When we met, I noticed she had lost weight, and I could immediately see the sadness in her eyes. I knew the weight loss was caused by grief. She had her hair cut in a new, shorter style and had lost the highlights, letting her natural blond shine through. We found a quiet corner in the back near a display of red and white holiday mugs.

"I know this will sound…contrived," I began. "But I'm sorry. Not that everything was exposed, but I'm sorry that it happened and that I hurt you."

The tears came to both of us at the same time. She nodded.

After a deep breath, she asked, "Why did it happen?"

I had to think, although I'd thought of that question a thousand times over the past year. I tried not to get distracted by the quiet chatter and festive laughter that emanated from every table in the shop and the piped in Christmas music.

"I didn't want it to happen. I didn't plan for it."

"Then why?" she pushed harder.

I wanted to protect her, spare her the answer. But I knew she deserved to hear what I knew to be true. Maybe some good could come from it. I stared into my black coffee and added cream.

"I felt disconnected from you. Like I wasn't needed much. You had the kids, and it was almost like you didn't need me. I wanted to be needed, I guess," I said as I leaned closer to her, trying not to let others close by hear.

Her tears came again, this time streaming down without sound. She made no attempt to wipe them away. Her blue eyes simply stared at me.

"Was she better than me? Did you love her?"

"In no way was she better than you. And...I suppose, at some time, I loved her. At least, I was caught up in the feeling of love."

"But it wasn't your fault, Beth," I continued. "It was me. I think, looking back, that I wasn't happy with who I was. I wasn't ever searching for another person, another woman. I was frustrated that I couldn't be the man I thought you needed at the time. I got short with the kids. They pushed all my buttons."

"That's what kids do," she said, not quite smiling. She wiped a few stray crumbs off the table with her hand.

"But it was more," I replied. "I was searching for that person I was when we first fell in love. Happy, content, fun-loving, looking forward to the future. Somewhere, I'd lost that. I don't know where—or how. And Jean—and she provided that. I thought. Then I realized she never loved me. She only loved the part of me that you held. She wanted to take that away from you. And when she couldn't—I never lost love for you—she lashed out."

"What a horrible person," my wife whispered.

I wanted to defend her but resisted. I nodded. "But I was worse because I let my selfish longings—really, a search for a new me or the old me—destroy us. I'll never get over that. It will live with me forever. And I'll be sorry forever."

We sipped coffee, and the conversation stalled. The crowd had thinned out, and the crew cleaned the counters and cleared the tables. It was time for her to go. I wanted to say I still loved her, that I was ashamed and remorseful. I tried to speak, but my throat closed tight on me. I only had my eyes to convey my feelings.

She stood. But I stayed in a subservient position and bowed my head, shaking it slowly. She reached down and touched my outstretched hand. We stayed in that pose, neither of us moving. I didn't want her touch to end.

"Forever is too long to suffer," she said.

I looked up and saw hope in her eyes. My heart began to beat again.

Book Two

DYING

Gravesite Service

"I don't think I know you. Were you a friend of my wife?" he asked in the foyer of the church.

I nodded.

"George Gray." He stuck out his hand.

"Nice to meet you," I said, shaking.

"And you are…?"

"Just a friend of your wife."

We stared at each other for a few beats longer than was comfortable.

Finally, he said, "There's a reception at our house after the gravesite service. Do you know the address?"

I nodded again. I didn't want to tell him I had it memorized. Then he walked away, and I detected a slight shake of his head. Maybe I imagined it.

After the service and without an invitation, I followed the procession from the church to the cemetery. I'd come this far, might as well see it through to the end.

When family and friends gathered close, I slouched in the back row. I noticed George look at me and say something to the young woman sitting next to him. Dressed in black, tears running down her cheeks, she looked back at me and shook her head.

After the "dust to dust," the young girl who'd been crying approached me. The crowd was scattering quickly, as they usually do at gravesites.

"Hi," she managed to squeak out.

"Hi, there."

"I'm Callie."

"Tom."

Then I saw a familiar look in her eyes. "You're the daughter, right?"

She nodded.

Her big brown eyes had the exact same shape as her mother's. But her coloring was way off, nothing like her mom. Maybe like her dad, but I didn't get a good look at him and I'd been picturing her mom for thirty years.

"Yeah, you look a lot like your mom. Better than looking like your dad."

She looked stricken by my words. I'd offended her. "I love my dad."

I wanted to say *I loved your mom*, but I resisted. "Sorry, I tried to make a compliment. It...it kinda came out wrong."

She got this squinty look in her eye and then recognition ran all over her like a waterfall. Her mouth dropped open. "You're him, aren't you?"

I just took a deep breath, no nod, no acknowledgement.

"Tom...Tommy, right?"

"Yeah."

"Oh, my, what are you doing here?" she asked, looking around, swiveling her head one way and another, like she didn't want anyone to overhear.

"I saw the announcement on Facebook. I was close by."

She looked down and kicked a pebble with her shoe. When she glanced up, she asked, "You live around here?"

"Arizona."

"Arizona? That's gotta be like a thousand miles away."

"Three hours by plane," I offered.

She swiveled her head back to the crowd breaking up. "You coming to the house?"

"Nah. Sounds too much like a party." I wanted nothing to do with her dad. I hated him in that way that you make up in your mind, even though you've never met the person.

"God, I can't stand it," she said, tears spilling down her

cheeks.

I had nothing. No comfort to offer. No hand on the shoulder, no hug.

"I need a drink. You wanna buy me a drink at a bar I know?" Her words came out like a demand, or maybe a dare.

I wanted none of that scene, but I said, "Sure. I'm a little dry myself."

"I'm in the white Mazda. Follow me," she gestured and started walking away.

So, I did.

The bar wasn't exactly a dive, but it wasn't the country club either. In the middle of the day, only a few early risers littered the joint. That's what it was, a joint. Kind of funky, for the younger crowd, maybe even hip for Omaha. But I didn't notice much about the interior. My vision blurred in memories of her mom and a combination of dread and wonder about Callie.

We settled into stools at the end of a long wooden bar. She ordered a gin and tonic. I had a local draft beer.

"You look older than your photos," she said.

"I am." I jerked my head back. "Wait…you've seen photos?"

"Listen, cut the crap." She spun the barstool toward me and crossed her arms. "I'm in no mood. I know all about you and my mom. I was her confidant. Even though I didn't want to be. At least, until my dad turned into a butthead. Then she needed somebody to talk to."

"He sure looked like a butthead to me," I said, trying to get her to smile.

At first, she thought I was serious but then relented, smiled, and shook her head. "Mom always said you had a pretty wicked sense of humor."

We sat and sipped. I picked at the tiny pretzels in the plastic bowl in front of me, popping a few in my mouth. Finally, I said, "Won't you be missed at the *reception?*"

"Hardly."

"Why's that?"

"I'm officially the black sheep of the family. Just don't seem to fit in much."

"Sorry. But every family has one." I shrugged. "Pardon me for saying, but you don't look anything like a black sheep, with the possible exception of drinking gin in the morning."

"Gin in the morning, sailors take warning. Gin at night, sailor's delight."

Now it was my turn to smile, for the first time all day. Maybe all week.

"Why did you come all the way to Omaha to say goodbye to my mom?" she asked, the severity returning to her eyes.

I'd been asking myself the same question for the past two days. I hadn't figured it out completely except that it seemed like the exact place I should be, even without a reason. Finally, I said, "It has something to do with unfinished business. I guess I had to finish it. Saying goodbye, I mean."

"She always said you just ran away."

I wanted to protest, but...yeah...that was pretty much dead on. I reluctantly nodded.

"I had my reasons," I added without much vigor.

After another sip, she said, "I think she always loved you."

I didn't want to tell her I felt the same. I didn't know Callie well enough. She was having a pretty dreadful day, and I didn't want to contribute to it.

"She married your father. She raised three great kids, two white sheep and one black. Us, the two of us, me and your mom, that love was thirty years ago."

"That's not the way I heard it."

I knew what she was talking about, but I couldn't bring myself to ask what she'd heard. So, I ordered another round.

"What? No reply?" Again, with that demanding voice.

"What do you want me to say? That I had an affair with your mom? If you already know that, you want an apology or something?"

"I want the truth!" she said in her best Tom Cruise imitation.

Then, "I love that movie," breaking the tension.

"I've been searching for the truth for the past twenty years. Not sure I know exactly what it is," I said.

"Just tell me about San Francisco," she replied, softness and sadness returning to her eyes. She motioned to the bartender for more pretzels.

I sighed and let out a breath, remembering. I focused on the muted TV behind the bar, the news headlines crawling slowly to the left.

"I'd been divorced a couple of years when she called. She said she was going to Frisco for a week. Wanted to know if I could fly up and say hello."

"Seems like you did way more than say hello."

"She was having trouble with your dad. Maybe realizing she was falling out of love—or at least having a hard time finding it with him. We all go through those times. Some of us act on it; others suffer through till the sunshine returns. If it does."

"Then why you?" she wanted to know.

"Like you said, I ran away. No closure. I suppose she wanted to find out if we still clicked. But there was no presumption of leaving your dad. That just wasn't her."

"So, you *clicked* with her for a week?" It wasn't really a question.

"And then she ran away. I never saw her again."

Callie started to cry again, first silently, tears running down her cheeks. Then little sobs erupted. I put my arm around her, and she pulled away but then slumped toward me. She smelled like orange blossoms.

"When was it?" she asked.

"What?"

"The trip to San Francisco."

I knew it by heart. "February 1995."

She stopped sobbing, took in a few quick breaths, then faced me and stared into my eyes. She had a faraway look, like she was looking past me and into me at the same time. Then her eyes widened, and she looked away quickly.

"What just happened there?" I asked, not sure I really wanted to know.

She shook her head like she was trying to dislodge a memory. Or forget one.

I pried a little more, but she gave up nothing. We ordered another round, and as we talked, I watched her. She had several mannerisms like her mom, especially her chuckle, which seemed to pop up often and continue until the next breath swooped in with an audible hiccup. I didn't want to leave, but her phone kept buzzing and I suspected it was her dad, wondering where she was.

We had talked mostly about her mom, like the quirky ways she got her kids to obey. Not quite bribery, but very incentive laden—and with a steely determination to not be fooled. The similar trait that I'd seen in Callie. She asked a few questions about my life, too. Kids (no, it never seemed to be the right time); jobs (plenty, mostly in manufacturing operations except for that stint as a private investigator); marriages (just one—it didn't last).

Finally, she was ready to go. She asked if she could stay in touch with me. I wanted to say no, that she should forget she ever met me. But I grabbed a coaster from the bar and wrote down my cell number and email address on the back.

We hugged when she stood to leave. She gripped me hard, not like a casual, just-met-you embrace. She tilted her head up and kissed me on the cheek, new tears in her eyes.

"I was born in late 1995," she said as she stood to go.

Then in a whisper, "Mom always said Callie was short for California."

A weird sound crept up my throat but only emerged as a tortured groan. I reached for her, but she'd slipped out the door. I threw three twenties on the bar and hustled after her.

Eleven Minus Nine

I raised one finger, which meant two more. One Blanton bourbon, one Bulleit rye. I'd lost count by then.

I drank mine with rocks and a splash, thinking I was getting at least a little water into my system. He drank his neat. I'd had a dull ache haloing my head for three days, like I'd been wearing a hat two sizes too small.

We hadn't said a word in ten minutes. Talked out over the past several days. The silence wasn't comfortable, but it was better than what I imagined our thoughts were.

We were thinking about death.

It was down to the two of us now. Our group had started out as eleven. Close friends, fraternity buddies, and, unlike most college relationships, we hadn't let go. We made it through the 1960s with sporadic correspondence. A wedding here or a reunion back on campus there.

Even when we scattered across the country, we kept up contact, if a little sporadic. Before cell phones and cyberspace, we managed Christmas cards and phone calls.

When the '70s rolled around, we finally figured out we hadn't made any better friendships, so we planned excursions to renew ours. A houseboat trip on a lake—we did that one every year until we got bored with cooking all our own meals. A dude ranch out West—three squares a day suited us fine. Until our knees, backs, and butts started to complain loudly. Vegas, Nashville, NYC, and Key West made the cut. Anyplace men could enjoy themselves without women was fine by us. No girls allowed.

We lost one early on—a drug overdose. Nancy Reagan's

slogan didn't cut it—*Just Say No* is a lovely, catchy, little two-bit phrase that holds no quarter in the real world. One down.

Two of us died on the inside first. No outside marks, no scars, nothing visible. But no flame in the lantern. They lost their passion for life. Delicate little diseases that shouldn't have killed them, they let overwhelm them. Don't complain, don't argue, just take it like a man. I know, I know, that's easy for me to say, but they didn't seem to fight too hard. Both died early, almost like they were ready for it to end. Maybe it beat the alternative, whatever that was in their own head. Two more down.

A train splattered one. A freaking train! We never got the whole story from his family. Something about trying to rescue the family dog stuck on the tracks. Don't get me wrong, I love the little pooches, but I never bought that. We all knew he struggled long and hard with depression, so we figured he walked in front of that train. What kind of hell must you be living through to let the front side of a freaking mile-long coal train deliver you to the Promised Land? I don't criticize the family for the dog story. They can invent fabrications to cover up tragedies, and if it makes it a little easier to swallow, have at it, I say. Who's it gonna hurt? The dearly departed? The dearly splattered?

I got a two-inch tattoo of train tracks on my left calf as a tribute. Or maybe just a grisly reminder of how close the train always is. To any of us. I still shiver anytime I think about it.

Cancer ate up three of us. All the money all the world has spent on cancer, and where are we? So many people dying, just like they've always died. Slow, horrible, painful deaths. And our treatment campaigns to fight back? Surgery, butchery. Or kill it with chemo—all the while hoping the poison doesn't kill us before it cures us. Medicine takes us to the edge of death and tries not to push us over. Two I couldn't even visit, it happened so quickly. The one I did see—on his deathbed—all I could think of was how glad I was that it wasn't me lying there.

How's that for friendship?

Then I was thinking that he might ask me to go find a gun

and end it sooner rather than later. Geez—if he'd have asked, I might've considered it. How's that for friendship?

One died in a car crash. One died when his heart exploded. Just luck of the draw, I suppose. Their time. They didn't have much to say about it.

If you're keeping track, now we're back to the two of us. The other guy, he's the one that played by the rules: married early, had kids, worked for one company for forty-odd years or so. Me? None of the above. No wifey, no kiddos, no pension. Never met a rule I couldn't break.

He's healthier than me. He's got a brand-new hip, and I'm hobbling from a motorcycle crash. He works out four times a week. I use that Bowflex I bought on MTV as a mannequin for the only sports coat I own. He eats paleo; I crave donuts. He detoxes three times a year. I'd hate to see my liver in a scan. He breathes clean air from his mountain home. I've seen my chest X-rays and they ain't pretty.

He's smarter than me, too. Got a master's and a law degree. I tried Dale Carnegie courses after college.

So, we sit on these barstools. We're hoping to hang on, win the race, outlast them all. But we really don't want to be sitting on the next barstool all alone. Neither of us wants to be the last one. But we don't want to be the next to last one either. But if you had to choose…

I suspect we're both thinking the same thing in this silence. *I think I'm stronger than he is.* Health has nothing to do with it. Wisdom neither. It's all about strength—the will to live.

As the halo tightens around my head, I slip one hand down and grab hold of the barstool, hanging on for dear life.

Tail Thumping

The Driver was running late. He'd been up since 4 a.m., hauling gravel from the pit to the work site, but he wanted to finish one more run. He punched the truck's accelerator and it groaned under the forced workload. If he could just pick up the pace, he could unload the truck and still make it on time to his second job as a swing shift janitor out in Manteca. With eastbound traffic at this time of day, it was cutting it pretty close. If he showed up late again, he could lose that second job, and he had bills to pay.

The old truck strained under the Driver's lead foot. Still, the freeway wasn't congested, so he pushed it just a little more.

The Woman loved her white Cadillac Escalade. Her armored car, as she liked to call it. It packed a lot of metal in a sweet package, something like 5,000 pounds, according to her husband. She felt snug and safe as it glided effortlessly down the freeway. Her two kids were asleep after hard days in school, buckled in tight, not dreaming, their faces turned away from the mid-afternoon sun. The Woman followed two cars behind the Driver.

As a blue, ten-year-old Toyota driven by the Teen under the influence of an ear-splitting rap anthem made an abrupt lane change in front of the Driver, he braked. Too hard and too suddenly, especially for his speed. His double-axle trailer with the load of gravel locked and began to skid to his left.

That started a chain reaction. The Guy in the black BMW to the left rear of the Driver's rig saw the truck begin to slide and slammed on his brakes. The Woman, trailing the BMW a little too close, hit her brakes hard. Her seat belt locked immediately as it was designed to do, preventing her from lurching forward in her seat or hitting the steering wheel directly.

But she had to pull hard to the left to avoiding hitting the BMW. Her left front fender clipped the center divide cement barrier with a shattering boom of metal scraping concrete, sending the Escalade spinning counterclockwise. At almost 70 miles per hour, the Woman saw her life spinning out of control. Several faces from her past flashed quickly before her eyes, and for a split second, time almost stood still as she tried to focus on one face after another. The face of her maternal grandmother was the last image transmitted, and it was abruptly obliterated, exploding into flashes of light, sound, metal, and concrete.

A late model Buick, its driver reacting slowly to the impending catastrophe, slammed into the driver's door of the Escalade, whiplashing the Woman from right, to left, to death. She died in an instant, the time it took her spinal cord to snap. Her two kids weren't so lucky.

Young Boy, age nine, tow-headed and into baseball, Xbox, and golden retrievers, rode in the passenger seat. He was sandwiched by that armor-clad SUV and the back of the Driver's trailer. It took him a little over ten minutes to die from a combination of traumatic head and internal injuries. His seven-year-old sister, Young Girl, actually made it out of the demolished SUV alive but died in the hospital barely twenty minutes after she arrived.

The accident site shut down the freeway for more than four hours and played havoc with the afternoon commute and the nerves of over 10,000 commuters. Caltrans, the California state agency responsible for highway maintenance, spent the majority of those four hours sweeping up the loose stones from the overturned gravel truck.

The Guy in the black BMW was trapped in his vehicle for more than two hours but escaped with a lacerated face, a broken left arm, and a shattered kneecap. He considered himself lucky, or maybe blessed. He promised God he would pray more often. The

Old Geezer in the Buick spent twenty-five days in the hospital with a number of injuries. His airbag was credited with not only breaking his nose but also saving his life.

The Teen in the Toyota never checked his rearview mirror and only learned of the accident later that evening while checking Instagram.

The Driver escaped injury but never made it to his second job that evening. His boss fired him the next day.

The Man married to the Woman suffered more than almost anyone else. Even more than the victims who survived the accident. They eventually healed and resumed their lives.

The Man tumbled down into despair and set up Camp there. There were times he never left the Camp, times he'd rather be there than anywhere else. He felt he had no reason to return to the world up there. He had no Woman, no Young Boy, no Young Girl.

All he had was Dog. And the darn mutt only reminded him of everything he'd lost out on that freeway. So, the Man ignored Dog. It seemed to always be in the way, silently at his foot, tail wagging incessantly. Staring at the Man but unable to speak or to comfort or rage against all that felt dead.

After several days, he emerged from the Camp momentarily and realized Dog needed food and water because the mutt was lying on the kitchen floor in front of his bowls, whining a bit, tail wagging, swishing back and forth along the tiles like a metronome. Those big brown doggy eyes followed the Man wherever he stumbled along in the kitchen and expressed something the Man couldn't see.

But the Man could see the pee spots. He swore, out loud, loud enough that Dog jumped up and backed into the corner of the room, far away, no wagging tail, no big brown doggy eyes.

The Man took a deep breath and stared at Dog, who didn't look up for much longer than his usual. He dropped his head even lower and slouched down, his paws like skis, skidding and snowplowing out in front, belly along the tile. The Man kept staring and staring.

After a very long time, at least in doggy seconds, Dog met the Man's eyes and his tail did a back and forth and back again but only that, no more.

The Man swore again, softer, and reached for the paper towel. Muttering, swearing, cleaning, mopping incessantly, the tile tortured by the repetition, the mop straining under the pressure, bellowing. Then he returned to his campsite, leaving Dog to his own little encampment in the kitchen close to the bowls.

Every day, Dog would lumber upstairs and stand at the door of Young Boy's room. He never entered. He would look each way, searching the room as much as he could, sniffing for a sign, any sign. Some days, he would lie at the door all day long. The next day, Dog would go to Young Girl's room. Same thing: look, sniff, check but never enter. If Dog was lucky, some days when he sat in front of Young Girl's room, the sun hit the floor just right and provided him with a slowly creeping sunbath. He would lie down and feel the warmth. When the bath finished, Dog would return to the kitchen where his bowls were.

In the rest of the house, minutes never moved, the clock of the Man's life stopped, busted, sprung. Days seemed to stretch out unbearably before slowly clicking off to the next one on the calendar. A week took a month to pass, maybe two.

The Camp gathered dust and dirt and bile and stink and sludge and ash and mud and mosquitos and lice and snakes and anger and hate and loathing. But not tears. They were forbidden in the Camp.

The Man returned to the kitchen every day, doggie weeks to Dog. Bowls got filled, and the tail began to wag like a metronome but stopped dead when the eyes surveyed the campsite messes, like someone's hand on the metronome, gripping hard, holding it silent.

Eventually, the Man began to leave the Camp, every morning, nine o'clock but not sharp, and returning every evening. Dog was never asked to join the Man in the upper Camp, now banished by spring-loaded gates to the tile of the kitchen.

One day when the Man returned to the kitchen, Dog didn't stand up. His eyes didn't catch the Man with hope and sadness. The tail never moved. Dog simply lay there, barely breathing. Doggy vomit scattered the tile like miniature bombings. The Man swore again but without hostility.

He lifted Dog, all limp, tongue hanging, paws twitching, into the car and began to drive. He knew the route; he'd driven it many times before the Woman and the Young Boy and the Young Girl had left him alone in the Camp, forever ago. The car seemed almost to drive itself, with Dog lying in the front seat, a soft and guttural moan filling the car. The Man noticed the stink of the Dog for the first time. At a stoplight, he looked down, catching the Dog's eyes for a bleak second, but concentrating on the fur, fur-balled and slick, not shiny and bright like he remembered. The Man began to hear the sound of the moan, to smell the stink of the fur, to see the darkness in the eyes, to see the lifeless tail. He increased his speed, running the reds, not stopping at the yellows, and speeding through the greens.

He had called ahead but still had to wait in the room, the room that was filled with cages and crates and leashes and yips and hisses. The one that smelled like a cocktail concoction of vitamins and Lysol. The waiting room with animal magazines and racks of organic treats and teeth cleaners and in the distance, files stacked behind the reception desk, each a dog or cat or bird or…no, no reptiles.

The Man lifted Dog, all fifty pounds of it, lighter than he remembered, like the last time he brought him here. He carried Dog into a tiny room with a cabinet, two chairs, and a shiny metal shelf anchored to the wall. He carefully placed Dog on the not-really-a-table, and the procedures began. Dog didn't like the temperature taking but had not the dignity or strength to complain. Then, teeth examined, breath scrutinized, charts ticked off, and ready for the next human to look at Dog.

The Vet opened the back door to the room, the door that led

to someplace neither the Man nor Dog, presumably, had ever been or ever wanted to go

The Vet gently stroked Dog, head to tail, back and forth, and again. He was dressed in a white doctor coat and blue jeans and smelled about the same as everything else in the entire facility. He had a wonderful shelfside manner, all smiles and concern and gentleness. The Vet mostly ignored the man and concentrated on Dog. He stroked and stroked. He massaged Dog's head and rubbed his long snout, and he scratched behind his ears and Dog finally licked him. The Vet smelled his licked hand and almost imperceptibly nodded his head. He kept a slight smile and continued feeling and prodding and lifting and poking.

The Man was standing away from the shelf-table, leaning against the wall of the tiny room, his fists clenching, throat squeezing, eyes burning, breath gulping.

Dog lifted his head and searched the room, swiveling up and back, looking for the Man. The Vet smiled and motioned for the Man to come closer. He grabbed the Man's hand and placed it on Dog's head. And the Man massaged and rubbed and scratched. Dog laid his head back down on the metal, and his tail rose and gave one thump on the metal, sounding more like a bang.

Then one more bang. And another.

The Vet said he'd be right back. That he had to go into that back room. That Dog was sick and needed medicine and a needle and rest and water and food and time and lots of scratches and rubs and stokes.

The Man took his first breath in an hour. He pulled the chair close to the metal shelf, on the side where the Vet had been so he could look Dog in the eyes.

He put his face close to the long snout. Dog managed to lick the Man's nose once and bang the shelf-table four times.

The Man leaned closer, and his tears began to drip on the metal, pinging almost silently, pooling. Dog banged the shelf-table more.

The following week when Dog came home, he gingerly

jumped into a new fluffy bed in the kitchen. The Man carried him up the stairs and showed him another new fluffy bed next to the Man's bed.

The kitchen smelled like doggy treats and Pine-Sol. The Camp had been disassembled, torn down. Dog slept in the bedroom that night, dreaming new dreams. The Man slept through the night with no visitors from the Camp. When morning came, he reached down to rub and scratch and stroke. Dog thumped and thumped.

The Last Phone Call

I didn't recognize the phone number, but since I'd been doing work with a new client, I answered the call.

Big mistake.

"Hi," was all she said.

I wanted to say that if I'd known it was her, I wouldn't have answered, but we'd traveled down that road so many times before with no escape. I said, "Hi, there."

"I thought you didn't answer the phone if you didn't know the number?"

I was restrained. Maybe I'd matured in the past several years, but I doubted it.

Instead, I said, "Whose phone is this?"

"Just a friend's."

"How are you?" I finally asked.

"I'm sober, if that's what you mean."

It was, but I said, "No, that's not what I meant. But good for you."

"Forty-one days now, but who's counting."

"Double good. I'm glad. You sound good."

A few beats of silence. Where was this headed?

"I'm sorry, Jimmy."

"For what?"

"Everything, I guess."

"That about covers it all."

Silence now, creeping into the conversation, elongating the gaps. I didn't really want to know specifics. After all, I had work to do and it was a Wednesday. That didn't show much kindness, but then, we hadn't shown each other a speck of kindness since the divorce. So, I let the silence linger a bit.

"Jennifer? You still there?"

"Are you sorry, Jimmy?"

"I'm sorry for a lot of things." But I wouldn't get specific.

"That doesn't cover anything."

Just because she's finally sober and calls me on a Wednesday in the middle of the day, I'm supposed to say I'm sorry? My bad? Not happening.

More silence.

"What do you want, Jen?" I said, trying to soften my tone by shortening her name.

"I want to know it wasn't all my fault."

But it was, I wanted to say. I clenched my teeth, holding back those words. "We've been through all this before. Do we have to rehash it now?"

"If not now, when?" she countered. "I need to know I'm not a terrible person, that sure, I made mistakes, but that it wasn't all my fault. The breakup, the divorce, all that."

"You've been seeing a new counselor, haven't you?" I knew it was mean before it left my mouth, but her language reeked of counselor talk that would give her a way out, a leg up. She could get her self-esteem back—and center the blame on me.

"That was low," she muttered.

I just couldn't let it go. "It just seems that every time you find a new counselor and explain what happened to our life together, somehow I become the villain. They usually take the woman's side. Especially if they're a woman and the man isn't even there to defend himself."

"I never describe you as the villain. I know my mistakes. Most were mine. Okay, I suppose all were mine. But I apologized. I thought we could work it out."

"That was a long time ago, in a galaxy far, far away."

"I'm a little fragile right now, Jimmy. That language really doesn't help much." She sighed. "I know we've been down this road, but I get the feeling that everything hasn't been said."

Really? I thought. I got the feeling that everything had been said way too many times already.

"I think we held things back, our feelings maybe, our regrets. I have a lot of regrets, you know. I'm just trying to get them out."

"And I guess I'm saying that it's a little late for that. I know your regrets, Jen. You said them at the time. Or at least I understood them if you didn't verbalize them. We don't need to torture ourselves again with all this, do we?" I know I didn't.

Silence. Either she didn't know how to answer or didn't want to.

"I still love you, Jimmy," she finally said. "I never stopped."

"You often had a funny way of showing that," I countered, like a punch. I backed away from delivering the whole blow—the "indiscretions" as they became known between us.

She was silent a beat too long before she managed, "It was a very tough time in my life. I was struggling."

I wanted to point out that she was right, that she was so young when we married. That she had no idea who she was or what she wanted. But I knew, without admitting it to myself—at least not out loud—that that described me, too. During the breakup, I'd thought about myself when I tried to analyze what went wrong. But she was right about one thing. I didn't want to accept blame. She did all the bad things. It was so easy to make her the bad girl. Because she was. Outwardly, at least.

She continued. "If I had it to do over again, Jimmy, I'd do it so differently."

"Maybe, Jen. But maybe you didn't know how to do it at the time, so you just did the best you could." I should have stopped there, but the arrow had already been loaded, so I fired away.

"Your best just wasn't very good."

I heard her breath catch, like a big inhale, then a sob. Now my shoulders slumped, and I sighed, regretting every word.

"I'm sorry," I eventually said.

The ensuing silence roared in my ear.

"Why do we do that to each other?" she asked without blame.

"Old habits die hard."

"Stop with the clichés. Really, stop. It's beneath you, and you're better than that. Do you really hate me so much that you can't even tell me the truth?"

I wanted to say that she took away a part of my life and made it miserable. But I'd made her life miserable, too. I sighed again.

"I don't hate you. I hate what we became during that time. I'm trying to move on, put it behind me. Maybe...you should, too." It came out like a question, but I meant it as a suggestion.

"This is the only way I know how to 'put it behind me.' Which, by the way, is another cliché. Just saying."

"Jennifer, you cheated on me." There, the truth poking its head above the banter. The big, bad, ugly beast ready and willing to devour us both. "Do you understand how that...crushed me? How totally laid flat I was? It's the only thing you could have done to make me stop loving you. The only thing. Do you get that?"

"Yes." Barely audible. "But Jimmy, you cheated on me, too."

"What? I did not. Never. Why would you say a thing like that?"

I was confused, and I felt my breath quicken.

"I didn't mean physically," she said. "I meant emotionally. You weren't available to me when I needed you."

"You're absolutely right. After you cheated, I wanted nothing to do with you."

"I don't mean then. I mean before."

"Before? What are you talking about?" She was turning this into something I wasn't liking. I was the villain again.

"Your work, your sports, your friends. Sometimes I felt ignored. Invisible."

I was 23. What did I know about making a woman feel loved? But I couldn't say that. I didn't dare. So, I stayed silent—it was my defense, my shield, my shelter.

"Jimmy, I'm not blaming you. Not trying to make you the

bad guy. We both had no idea. We just fell in love, then fell into marriage. I suppose there were a lot of parts in between that we never figured out."

A wave of regret swept over me. I closed my eyes and tried to look at our past together.

"Yeah, you're right about that. But I still say that's…water under the…it's yesterday's news…I don't know, it just seems like we can never go back there. We have to move on. Start new."

"Without each other." She finished my thought.

I wanted to say that she hurt me too bad to ever forgive her, that I'd sealed off that part of my heart and it was never going to heal. That I didn't want it to.

Instead, with a deep breath, I said, "Yeah."

Now she started to cry, and she didn't hold back. Sobbing, gulping air. I could picture her now on the other end of the line—hair a mess, makeup running, nose sniffing, tears flowing. I wanted to reach through the phone and hug her, wipe the tears away, anything I could do to ease the pain. But it brought pain to me, too.

I remembered all those late nights when I didn't know where she was and she'd come home late, smelling…different than she should. That's the first thing I noticed. Also, I could see something in her eyes, but I couldn't name it. It turned out to be guilt. But guilt was not even on my radar at the time. I had no conception that when we lay together naked in bed that she could possibly do that with another man. Somebody other than her husband.

As soon as she saw me noticing these differences in her, she'd change the subject dramatically. She'd talk about a new dishwasher or a trip to New York City that she'd always wanted to take or a new outfit she coveted but knew we couldn't afford or a…this…or a that…anything to cover her tracks. But I wasn't looking for a trail. I was trying to figure out what was happening, how it was all so different than the first year of our marriage. I was confused, lost. I couldn't talk about it with my sister or my mom or dad or my buddies. Jen wouldn't talk, not about the real issue of her actions, or her heart, or whatever it was that let her do what she did. So, I struggled alone.

That's what we do, isn't it? We struggle alone, thinking that our strength or intelligence or resolve is enough. It wasn't. It rarely is.

She stopped crying. I didn't want to think her crying was staged just to pry into my heart. I could feel her pain even through the telephone line. It felt real, stabbing at my heart, nicking a blood vessel, bleeding internally. I wanted to sympathize or at least tell her I understood. But I couldn't.

"I think we're done here, right?" I said. Then, trying to soften the blow, "For now?"

"It'll never be done for me, Jimmy. Just give me a second to…" her voice trailed off.

Her way of communicating back in our marriage often took this kind of path. A bit, a sliver, then nothing. My imagination had often taken over. It wasn't hard to do—imagining her not in love with me. In love with another man. At least involved with somebody else. Nothing she ever said made me think this way. My mind just took over and led me down that dark road. Or she would say something innocuous—like she felt lonely—and I would think she was saying that I wasn't enough for her. I couldn't fill some void I never even knew she had. Maybe she didn't know it either. Maybe loneliness wasn't even what she was feeling. Maybe it was sadness or depression or hopelessness.

I didn't want to admit that her loneliness was my fault. If she felt lonely around me, what did that say about me?

At first when she admitted the affair, I was stunned into a dark void, blackness. I drew back, filled with rage about everything. Her, him, me even. Me? Yes, I was raging against myself because I witnessed my marriage failing. That wasn't supposed to happen to me. Not me. Never.

I left for a week—headed to the coast. Slept in the van for a few nights and then found a fleabag. I don't remember eating much at all that week and was shocked when I got back that I dropped almost ten pounds.

When my boss called and told me to get back to work, I almost quit on the spot. But I went back to work and to Jennifer and the crushing silence in our home. I couldn't speak without revealing my anger. She couldn't reply without guilt overwhelming her. She never had many women friends to confide in, and her mother showed no signs of empathy—ever. My mom was addicted to painkillers for her arthritis, and she'd never been much for hearing any of my secrets. Dad was aloof and working on his golf game in retirement.

We tried counseling, but I was impatient with the process. Working on my past—and her past—seemed like a waste of time. How we were brought up and the way our families communicated was all nice to know, but that didn't really help in our sorrow and grief. Our marriage was crumbling, and the counselor—female of course—wanted to talk about our childhoods? Give me a break. I lasted four sessions, and Jen kept going, switching counselors when the process bogged down, as it always did.

Finally, after six months of torture, I moved to an apartment across town, bought a new pair of running shoes, and hammered out long, methodical runs. It gave me a goal, this getting in shape, and I suppose it was kind of a self-flogging mechanism to punish myself—even though I didn't know why I needed punishing. Jen took to the bottle. She'd always had a weakness there, and for a while in our early days together it was fun when she'd get a little tipsy. Whenever she'd start to drink too much and too often, she knew how to back away. Now, she'd seemed to lose that awareness, and she'd call, late in the evening, slurring her words. I started hanging up on her.

I got in shape, worked extra-long hours, and kept to myself. Jen entered rehab, twice. I felt superior, handling this separation so gallantly, toning my physical self and almost totally neglecting my emotional health. I could tough this out. I still wasn't talking to Jen much, but I did manage to show up at the hospital the first time she went into treatment. Not the second time. I did call a few times though.

The sound of her blowing her nose into the phone brought me back to today.

"I'm sorry. I didn't mean to do that in front of you," she said, still sniffling.

"It's okay, Jen," I replied, a little too condescending, even to my ears.

"Thanks."

"Listen," I said. "I need to get back to work now."

That silence again.

Finally, she said, "When can we talk again? Can we get together?"

"You can call me again, but I don't really think getting together is going to get us anywhere."

She said nothing. I waited, knowing I'd hurt her further but unremorseful.

"Jen, are you there?"

"I'm not sure I want to go on without you," she said in a voice I'd never heard before.

"I'm no prize, Jen. I'm really not," I said, trying to diffuse the comment. "I'm not sure I even know anything about myself. I feel pretty lost right now, and I know I'm not a good partner. Okay, I take responsibility for my part in the marriage. Maybe I wasn't any good. Maybe I was a terrible husband. I didn't communicate. I didn't understand. I felt horrible, betrayed, and I'm sure I took it out on you. To tell you the truth, I don't know if I'll ever be any good again."

I felt better after my mini catharsis. I couldn't give her what I thought she needed—hope—I could only tear myself down. Maybe that would make her feel better, to soldier on.

But she was silent.

"See," I continued, "I'm no good for you."

In a whisper, "You'll never convince me of that. Never."

Then she hung up.

Two weeks later, her sister found her dead in our home, an apparent overdose.

I would never hear her voice again, never get another phone call.

I finally cried.

Release the Red Snowballs

"You look sad today, Gretchen," Tommy said. The two sat on the playground grass, and he held a small truck in his hand.

She looked up and frowned

"That's because my momma's sad."

"Why is she sad?" he asked, looking at the truck but not making it push dirt or unload what he imagined it had gathered.

"I'm not sure."

"She didn't tell you? Did you ask her?"

"She and my papa tried to explain it to me, but I really didn't know what they were talking about. Something about a man named Luke."

Tommy had an uncle named Luke, but he lived far away, and he was pretty sure Gretchen wasn't talking about him.

"Is Luke your uncle or something?" he asked.

"No. He's a disease."

Tommy knew that word. His momma used it whenever he didn't feel good. But he didn't know any man like that.

"Like a bad man or something?"

"Yes, very bad, according to my momma. And he's in my body. He invaded my body."

That didn't make any sense to Tommy. He wanted to ask how a man could be inside the body of his friend, but he didn't even know how to ask. And he didn't want to sound dumb to her. He'd liked Gretchen ever since he saw her in first grade, and he would rather play with her than some of his buddies. At least most of the time.

He knew one way to try and comfort her. "My papa is a doctor. Maybe he can...find a way...to make you all better."

She brightened at that. "But I already have a doctor. He wears a white coat."

"My papa is a special doctor. Is your doctor special?"

She shrugged.

"Maybe that would make my momma feel better, too," she finally said.

Tommy smiled back at her. "My papa can make anybody feel better. He's the best doctor ever. Just you wait and see."

Then Tommy remembered that he and Gretchen had promised not to tell their secrets to anyone. Not even their mommas and papas. They made that promise to each other the day they had held hands in line at the museum on the field trip. Nobody had noticed and they didn't think it was wrong, but still they made a pact not to tell anybody. Forever and ever.

"Can I tell him about this man Luke?" he asked, picking up the truck and inspecting the wheels.

"Yes," she whispered, "but only him. Okay?"

Tommy nodded and put the truck back on the ground and began to imagine it pushing a big load of dirt off the playground grass.

That evening, Tommy's momma hunched over the kitchen sink, finishing up the dinner dishes. She rolled her neck first to the right and then to the left and cocked her head in that direction and held it there. Then she pushed her chin to the sky. As she contorted her head in all directions, Tommy's papa looked up from his newspaper.

Tommy colored in his Spiderman book alongside his papa at the dining room table.

"When you're done, come join me on the couch," Papa said

to his momma as he moved to the nearby sofa.

"Can I come, too?" Tommy asked.

"Sure, buddy." Papa pointed to the coffee table in front of him. "You can color here if you promise not to get crayon marks on the table."

"I promise," Tommy said, sitting on his knees in front of the wooden table.

Momma ruffled his hair as she plopped down beside her husband.

"Long day?" he asked as he grabbed her hand and kissed it. Tommy knew it smelled like the coconut lotion she always added after doing the dishes.

She nodded and began to stretch her neck again.

"Headache?" he asked.

"Yes, Mr. Wizard, care to dissolve it for me?" Momma answered, smiling directly at him.

"It's my heart's desire, my love."

"Just so you know, it's not one of those migraines. I haven't felt one of those in a long time. This is just a stress headache. Long day at work, you know?"

Tommy kept coloring but looked back at his parents often.

"Get comfortable," Papa instructed. "And take a few deep breaths. Again."

His momma lay back against the cushions and began breathing deeply as Tommy stopped coloring and turned to watch. He'd seen this before, but somehow it seemed more important after his talk with Gretchen on the playground.

"Tell me precisely where your head hurts," Papa asked.

"On the right side, starting at the top of my scalp and extending all the way into my neck and along my shoulder."

"What color is it?"

"Black," she immediately answered.

"What shape is it?"

"That's a hard one. It's like a flat piece of paper, black construction paper, crumbled on both ends. And another piece of smaller paper along my neck."

"Is the shape thick or thin?" Papa asked. "Describe the depth of the shape."

"About four or five inches thick."

"Okay, good. We have the location, color, and shape. Now, let's see if anything has changed. More deep breaths, please."

Tommy had turned completely around and was sitting on the table, looking first at Momma and seeing the pain on her face. Then he looked Papa, whose eyes were pointed toward the ceiling. Tommy turned around to see what his papa might be looking at.

"Now tell me where the pain is," Papa said again.

Momma hesitated this time, and her head shifted, first to the right, then to the left. "It's now on my right side from the top of my head to about my right ear."

Tommy saw the pain in Momma's face go away.

"What color is it?"

"Green, emerald green."

"What shape?"

"A rectangle, but not too thick, maybe an inch or two."

This time, Momma took a few more deeps breaths without any instruction from Papa. Tommy remembered her saying something about it wasn't her first rodeo the last time she did this, but he didn't know what horses had to do with a headache. He'd ask later, when this was all over, but he knew better than to interrupt when Papa was at work.

"Now how big is it?" Papa asked.

"About the size of a baseball. But flat."

"And the color?"

"Yellowish."

"Location?"

"Just at the side of my head near my right ear."

Another pause was punctuated by more deep breathes.

"Size?" Papa asked, looking directly at her but keeping still.

"Golf ball."

"Color?"

"White," Momma said.

"Location?"

Momma didn't answer. Tommy saw her turn her head back and forth, back and forth.

Finally, she said, "The location is gone." She leaned over to give Papa a kiss. Tommy turned away, smiling.

"I love when you do that, thank you so much," she said, snuggling close to him and clasping his hand in hers.

"Heart's desire." They kissed again, and Tommy colored a girl that Spiderman was talking to, giving her emerald green hair.

Later that evening, Tommy lay on his bed with his papa beside him. From his back, he looked up at the ceiling and the underside of a book that his papa was reading. Every character in the story sounded different as Papa read faster and faster, like a roller coaster running down the tracks, gaining speed.

After the story, Tommy and his papa usually talked about their day. Tommy would share something about school and his papa would share something—and it often sounded like magic—that happened in his medical practice. When the talking was done and Papa suspected that Tommy was drifting off to sleep, his son asked a question that started them into a brand-new conversation.

"Is a headache a disease?" Tommy asked.

"In a way, yes, I suppose you could call it a disease. But usually a small one that goes away quickly."

Tommy looked like he wanted to ask the next question, but he had trouble putting it into words.

"Why do you ask, son?"

"You know my friend Gretchen? She has a disease."

"I'm sorry to hear that," his papa said, sliding down next to Tommy. "Did she say what kind of disease?"

He nodded. "She said her disease was a man named Luke and that he had invaded her body."

"Luke, huh? Does Luke have a last name, Tommy?"

"Yeah, Gretchen thinks it's 'creamy'."

"Creamy like ice cream, that kind of creamy?" Papa asked.

Tommy nodded again but was having trouble keeping his eyes open.

Papa didn't say anything more, but he was frowning like he usually did when he was thinking really hard. His pulled the covers up to Tommy's chin and turned off the light.

The next morning at breakfast, Papa suggested that Tommy invite Gretchen over to their house after school to play and to stay for dinner. Momma would call Gretchen's mother and make all the arrangements. Tommy said he'd like that very much. And so, the arrangements were all set. Papa said he had an idea.

Mama made meatloaf, mashed potatoes, and green beans for dinner. After they ate, they went into the TV room and they all settled on the floor. Papa said he had a game he wanted them to play.

"Let's play a game of good guys versus bad guys. It's a game that's all imagination. You can make up anything you want, and you each can play. Okay?" Papa began.

Both kids looked at each other and shrugged.

"Oh, I forgot to tell you. This is a special magical game. Only you two can see the game, and it'll just be your secret. Sound good?" Papa asked, smiling.

This time, both kids sat up straight and smiled at each other.

"Now, let's figure out what to call the good guys."

"Goodies," Tommy shouted.

"Avengers!" Gretchen shouted a little louder.

Tommy liked that better, and they all agreed to call the good guys the Avengers. "Let's put the Avengers in red uniforms," Papa suggested. "Okay?"

Tommy looked at Gretchen, and both kids nodded enthusiastically.

"Now, what shall we name the bad guys?"

Gretchen and Tommy thought hard, their little faces scrunched up.

Suddenly, a name popped into Tommy's head. "The Meanies."

"That's a good one, Tommy," Gretchen said, patting him on the shoulder.

Papa looked like he wanted to smile.

"Okay, it's settled. The Avengers versus the Meanies," Papa declared. "Let's put the Meanies in white uniforms, okay?"

"Sure, like those bad guys in *Star Wars*," Tommy said. "Are the Avengers gonna go to war with the Meanies?"

"Oh, I don't like war," Gretchen said.

"Okay, I understand, not many people do, Gretchen," Papa responded. "Especially, little girls. Let me ask you a question. If you wanted to make sure the good guys, the red Avengers got rid of all the bad guys, the white Meanies, how do you see that happening?" Papa looked at Gretchen and put his hand up to keep Tommy quiet.

Gretchen put her hand under her chin and began to think. She squinted, and she looked off into the far side of the room. Tommy couldn't see what she was looking at. It was quiet in the den, so no sounds at all interrupted the game.

"I don't know," she finally said. Tommy let out a big sigh. He didn't know the answer either.

"Let me ask it another way. If we wanted to turn all the white guys into red guys, how would that happen?" Papa asked.

"Snowballs," Gretchen blurted out. "Red snowballs."

Tommy looked to his papa, and he nodded back at the boy.

"We could have a snowball fight. The Avengers could toss snowballs at the Meanies, and every time we hit one, they would turn red," Tommy said, smiling and feeling happy with his idea.

"Yes," Gretchen said. "We could make lots of snowballs and keep them in a red snowball fort and whenever we saw a Meanie coming at us, we could just throw a snowball and turn them all red."

"That's pretty cool. I like that," Papa said.

They spent the next half hour playing an imaginary game of Red Snowball. Tommy liked to lob snowballs in the air and see them fall on a Meanie, turning it red. Gretchen decided to roll the red orbs at the white guys, like bowling. They both liked building big red snowmen, and Tommy could see a giant snowman hurling the red snowballs every which way, like a robot with two arms rapid-firing snowballs. Gretchen just imagined these big red snowmen blocking the way for the guys in white, not letting them pass, like a patrol guard at school.

Papa watched the kids play their game as his idea began to take shape. Then he called an end to the game, and Momma served hot cocoa. They let the kids out in the snow to make a few real snowballs and throw them at a tree. She heard them yell "red snowballs" often. Tommy even asked if he could use the ketchup from the cupboard, but he couldn't persuade her.

Later, snuggling in bed with Momma, Papa whispered, "Now I have talk to her parents. I'm sure that Luke and creamy mean leukemia. They need to know what I know." That night, he seemed to dream in reds and whites.

A few days later, Papa came face-to-face with Gretchen's parents. He didn't know them well, having only exchanged several polite hellos at school functions.

After a few pleasantries, including letting them know that he knew about their daughter's condition, Papa began, "I'd like to work with Gretchen."

"We already have a physician," Gretchen's father said, suspicion in his voice.

"I'm not an oncologist, I'm a family doctor," Papa explained.

"Gretchen doesn't need another doctor," Gretchen's mother whispered. "Our daughter needs...a miracle."

"I believe miracles happen every day. Some we see, others go unnoticed because we are looking elsewhere," Papa said with his best bedside manner. "If you let me work a bit with Gretchen, I won't promise miracles, but I've been developing techniques to approach disease from a mental standpoint."

"A mental standpoint?" Gretchen's father said. "Our daughter is only seven years old. She doesn't have a mental standpoint."

Papa raised his hands as if defending himself. "Poor choice of words. I should have used the term 'imagination' in combating disease."

"Like what? You just imagine it goes away and poof, it's gone?" the father said, his eyes wide with mock wonder, his head bobbing from side to side.

Papa spent ten minutes explaining the power of the mind to heal the body. As Papa spoke in a low and melodious tone, Gretchen's parents began to calm and eventually ask questions.

"You really think this approach will work?" her mother asked.

"I've seen it work for minor ailments, but I've never tried it with cancer, so there can be no guarantees," Papa answered.

"I don't know if I can put myself through experimentation at this point. If we lose her…I'll simply die." Gretchen's mother began to sob, almost choking as she gulped air.

"I know how much you both love your daughter. Now you can show your love to an even greater extent, beyond perhaps anything you imagined. I will invite you to see what I'm doing with your daughter. She already shows the capacity of imagination that I believe can lead to healing."

"What do you mean, you've already begun to work with her?" the father asked, not so politely.

"No, no. We've just played an imagination game when she had dinner at our house last week. I can see Gretchen has the ability to visualize far beyond most children her age, my son included. It was simply an experiment to gauge how she might respond to this type of therapy. I can provide all the medical research documentation to share with your physician. He has already seen most of it, I assume. Although he may not see the benefit or interpret the design as I have—I've been working with it for years."

"I'm not sure," the father said. The mother continued to cry to herself, and Papa wondered if she'd lost the gist of the conversation.

"Speak to your oncologist," Papa said. "You have nothing to lose. And everything to gain. Just so you know, I've been captivated by your little Gretchen, as has my son. I'd do everything in my power to see her well again. And I'll keep our work secret, sharing it with no one. I'll include you in every session and give you weekly updates. All I ask in return is to see her blood work-ups occasionally to see if she's making progress." Papa waited for a reply.

Finally, Gretchen's father spoke. "Let me see the research."

Papa smiled.

One night, Gretchen's parents came to dinner. Momma had cooked chicken rice casserole with sliced apples and peaches on the side. She had apple pie warming in the oven, and it made the whole house smell good.

"Do both of you know how blood works?" Papa asked Gretchen and Tommy.

"It's the red stuff inside your body, right?" Tommy said.

Papa nodded

"It's like a river that runs through your whole body," Gretchen chimed in.

"That's a great way to describe it, darling," Papa said. "And what color is it?"

"Red!" they both shouted.

"And red is the color of...?"

"The good guys!"

Everyone smiled at their enthusiasm.

"It flows into every part of your body; did you know that?"

Papa continued. "Into the tips of your toes, and your nose. Into each finger and the top of your head. And every little nook and cranny." Papa began to point—and tickle ever so slightly—as he touched Gretchen on her back, her tummy, her kneecap, and her ear. He made her giggle.

"Sometimes," Papa explained, "bad things get in your blood. Like Luke Creamy."

Her parents both frowned in confusion but did not interrupt.

"And they're white," Gretchen said with a slight smile.

"Exactly," Papa exclaimed. "So, we have to make all those white Luke Creamys turn to red. Let's release the red snowballs!"

Snowballs? her father mouthed but did not say it out loud. To Tommy, he looked like he was thinking really hard.

The two kids mimicked throwing snowballs, and Tommy laid in the sound effects—*phew, phew, phew.* They both bounced in their chairs, with eyes closed, and they ducked every so often, like they were avoiding an incoming white snowball from the notorious Mr. Creamy.

"Now, let's build the fort to keep out all those white guys," Papa shouted. And the kids crouched in their chairs, their hands up now, patting together the make-believe shelter. Every so often, Tommy lobbed an unseen snowball at incoming menaces.

Papa let the kids have fun. Then his face changed like he had a new idea.

"Okay, now a new trick to battle the Meanies. I want you to see that great big fort you just built—and don't worry, you can build a new one. I want you to see it melt and flood in a rush of red water. And wash all the white Meanies away! Now! Melt it! Go!"

At first, the kids couldn't grasp the image. Then Tommy's sound effects came into play. *Whoosh! Whoosh!*

"Look out below," Tommy bellowed. "The dam has broken!"

Gretchen chimed in with a couple of softer *whooshes* herself.

"Now, look around," Papa instructed. "Do you see any white

Meanies?"

Both kids shifted their heads right and left and shook them back and forth. No more Meanies. Papa began to clap, slowly and rather quietly at first. Then Momma joined in. The clapping became louder as Tommy and Gretchen joined in, and soon everyone was rah-rahing with loud table-thumping and high-fiving.

Afterward, as Momma served piping hot apple pie with vanilla ice cream to the kids, Papa took Gretchen's mother and father outside into the crisp, cold night air. They all exhaled to see their foggy breath. Several stars shone, escorting the darker night to come.

"What just happened in there?" Gretchen's mother asked.

"It's a visualization technique I've used in my practice for years," Papa explained. "Patients see their bodies and the built-in defenses it generates, destroying the disease. In leukemia—Luke Creamy, in this case—the body produces too many white blood cells. If Gretchen can see her body produce more red cells and they overtake the white ones, maybe we can reverse the progression. Gretchen seems to be able to see that happen. That's the simple answer."

The look on her mother's face indicated to Papa that she did not yet believe.

"What do we have to lose?" Papa said, looking directly into her eyes.

"It might get her hopes up too high," she replied.

"Hope is exactly what she needs right now. The more, the better," Papa responded. "Let me work with her as you continue your regular treatment. No charge. I sincerely believe this can help cure her. And I think she is starting to believe it, too."

"I'm not sure I do," her father said.

"Fair enough," Papa conceded. "All I ask is that you not let her see your skepticism."

Papa waited for a reply, but none came. He continued, "Look, you gave me permission to speak with Gretchen's oncologist," nodding in the direction of her father. "I know her case now. I've familiarized myself with the exact issues with her blood. If I...if we...can generate more red blood cells to overtake the mutating white cells in her body, we can reverse this." Papa paused. "It's much more complicated than that, but then again, not really. Her body can heal itself; it just needs to get the right instructions from her. More red, less white, no mutations. In the meantime, you should continue with her treatment. If she were my child, I'd try every possible treatment. Every single one. I'm not advocating doing any less, I'm asking you to do more. Can you see the possibilities? And even if you can't, will you trust me? Will you trust me to help heal your wonderful little girl?"

Both parents simultaneously took in a breath, glanced at each other, then back at Papa. They nodded.

Not with much enthusiasm, Papa noted, but it was a start.

Over the next several months, Papa and Gretchen worked together twice a week. Tommy felt a little left out, but Papa assured him that even though he and Gretchen were working alone now, Tommy's help was still needed—and wanted.

Papa taught Gretchen to summon the good Avengers in their red uniforms every time she thought about it. Papa told Tommy to remind Gretchen whenever he could. Between the two of them, Gretchen increased the warfare of red over white numerous times a day, even though she preferred to still look at it as a snowball fight.

Despite Papa and Gretchen's work, her leukemia symptoms did not go away. Instead they got worse. She regularly missed days of school because she was too tired to go, missing an entire week in February. In March, just as it looked like spring may burst through the winter, Gretchen landed in the hospital to fight a nasty bronchial infection. Papa visited and found her tender to the touch and looking frail from weight loss. But he wasn't discouraged.

Papa studied Gretchen's blood work reports through her online medical records, grateful her parents had listed him as a member of her medical team.

On her eighth birthday, Papa, Momma, and Tommy attended a party in her honor at her home. Her parents and grandparents were the only others to attend. Gretchen lay on the couch the entire time, even to open presents and eat her cake. Her mother and father looked worse than she did, with fatigue etched all over their faces and with noticeable dark circles around their eyes, blackened by the unrelenting disease and fading hope. No light shone through their eyes.

After the party, Papa asked to see Gretchen alone in her bedroom. Her parents were hesitant at first but finally said yes.

As Papa sat on the edge of the bed, he looked deep into the little girl's eyes. He saw sadness, but he didn't think she'd given up.

"Now is the time, Gretchen," he began. She raised her chin and looked into his eyes.

"You've been too nice. To the Meanies. Now is the time they must be eliminated."

She had a worried look and began to breathe more quickly.

"I know," he continued almost in a whisper. "I know you haven't wanted to…destroy them. Just beat them back with a few red snowballs. It's not mean to destroy them. *They* are the Meanies!" his voicing rising now. "And they are making you feel bad. They must be put to…death, wiped away. They cannot stay any longer. Do you understand?"

She nodded but looked like she might cry.

"Yes, I know. It's scary. But you can do this. You can drive the Meanies away! Only you. You have the heart to do it, I know. You're a very, very strong young lady, even though you might not feel like it right now. You'll have help. All those snowballs you've got stored away in the fort? Can you see them?"

She closed her eyes and gritted her teeth. Then she nodded.

"And all those that Tommy made? Can you see them, too?"

Another nod.

"And can you see all the red rivers running through your body? All the good Avenger red rivers of your blood, into every part of your body. Your fingers. Your toes. Your ears. Your head, your tummy, your arms, your legs, your knees, your feet, your hands. Can you see those red rivers, child? Can you?"

"I can see them!" she shouted.

"Now, Gretchen! Now! Release all those snowballs! Release them! Flood the red rivers with all those snowballs! Go, child, go! Wipe away those Meanies. They are mean and nasty, and they do not belong in your body anymore!"

She was breathing hard now, concentrating all her inner strength.

"More, Gretchen! More snowballs. Release them all! Now! Now!" Papa was in a feverish stance, kneeling beside the bed, his fists balled tightly, one arm pumping up and down.

"Now, more flood, Gretchen! More flood! *Go, go!*"

"I will destroy you, you Meanies!" the little girl yelled.

Both her parents were now at her bedroom door. But they didn't enter. Her mother sobbed silently. Her father's fists were up against the door, and his head sagged between his outreached arms.

"More snowballs! Release the snowballs, Gretchen!" Papa shouted one more time. Together they continued to blast away at the Meanies, bringing all the resources the little girl could summon. Finally, she lay back on her pillow, exhausted. Papa unclenched his fists, breathed deeply, and nodded toward the young girl.

"Well done. Very well done," he said.

Three weeks later, at ten o'clock at night, Papa heard the phone ring. He thought it was a little late for a phone call. Only bad things are conveyed this late at night, he thought, as he reached for the phone.

"It's me," Gretchen's father said, his voice at a pitch Papa hadn't heard before. "Have you seen the latest blood work report?"

"No," Papa admitted. "I checked this afternoon, but it hadn't been posted."

"It was just added, ten minutes ago. It's time again," the father said. "It's time…right now! It's time to start making more snowballs!"

"Wha—" Papa asked.

"Because they're working. Those snowballs are working. Can you believe it? They are, I know they are."

The smile burst across Papa's face. "Hallelujah."

Author's Note

I've used the headache technique myself many times over the years within my family. Try it please; it works, especially on stress-related headaches. I first discovered the visualization technique depicted in this story in the writings of Bernie S. Siegel, M.D., beginning with his second book, *Peace, Love & Healing* (1989). Now retired from his medical practice and in his late 80s, his landmark work with many aspects of cancer treatment you may see as outside "accepted treatment techniques" and yet he has shown proven results. I hope his research continues; deadly diseases should be attacked with all the abilities within our arsenal.

Book Three

BELIEVING

Teen Jesus

"Have you seen our son?" the father asked the mother.

"What do you mean, have I seen him? Since when?"

"Since we left Jerusalem, since *then*?"

"Well, of course...he's probably with the other young boys. Right?"

"I'm not so sure. There're so many people. I just assumed he was with us, but I can't say for sure. He wasn't at our fire for dinner last night. Remember?"

The mother reviewed in her mind the past twenty-four hours or so. She retraced her steps and tried to remember the last time she saw their teenager. She remembered the large gathering as the caravan had stopped for the evening, lit the fires, and cooked the dinner meal. At bedtime last night, she didn't remember her son coming into the makeshift tent they'd erected.

"You go to the head of the caravan and start the search for him," she instructed her husband. "I'll head to the rear and do the same. Ask everyone you encounter if they've seen him. I'll meet you back here when the sun is at its daily peak. Go, go!"

After a frantic three-hour search, they reconvened where their donkey had been tied to the wagon in front of them. The caravan had not stopped to look for the boy because their small family of three was one of a great many on the road home from the pilgrimage.

"He's nowhere to be found," the father said, out of breath. "I asked everyone. You have any luck?"

The mother shook her head twice, slowly.

"Where could he possibly be?" he asked, vainly searching the immediate vicinity with his eyes.

"I have an idea," the mother said. "You get the donkey and several days' worth of supplies. Ask our neighbors to watch what little else we brought. If you could take two more men to accompany us, it would make the journey back to Jerusalem much safer."

"Jerusalem? That's over a day's walk," the father said. "Why do you think he's back there?"

"Mother's intuition. Go and do as I ask. We must leave now. We have several hours before sunset."

When they returned to Jerusalem, the couple and the two shepherds with them looked for the boy for three days. At the end of the third day, exhausted and hungry, the foursome decided to head back to the temple in search of bread and a place to bed down for the night. The town was almost deserted compared to the activity that had surrounded the Passover pilgrimage. Supplies were depleted by the throngs of people who had returned to their birthplace.

Worry and fatigue were etched across the faces of the parents, now after four days without sign of their son. The dust of the desert lined the perspiration streaks on their cheeks and necks. The poor carpenter didn't tell his wife that he had little money left and that their supplies were dwindling. The two shepherds held their heads low and wouldn't make eye contact.

As the mother climbed the steps to the temple and reached for the door, it burst open. There stood her son.

"Jesus," she said in a voice that startled the boy and made heads turn from the dozen people surrounding the holy site.

"Yes, Mother? What's wrong?" the boy answered. "There's no need to yell."

"Where in creation have you been for the past four days? We've been looking for you everywhere. We were frantic with concern. Why are you still here in Jerusalem?"

"Why were you worried? You should have known I'd be here

in the temple. Where else would I be? C'mon, Mother," Jesus answered with a shake of his head.

"Say what?" Mary replied, her eyes widening and her mouth tightening.

By now, the father had joined his wife and son at the top of the steps. He immediately grabbed his wife's hand as she leaned closer to the boy.

"You do not speak to your mother that way, young man. Understand?" Joseph said in a voice that settled his wife and made Jesus look down.

"But, Father—" the boy began.

"No buts, apologize now. We've been looking four days for you, and we are not in the mood for any back talk."

"I am sorry, Mother. But...uh...I have so much to do and learn, I thought more time in the temple would help me. You know how I get sometimes. I didn't mean to cause you and Father worry, but I needed to be here. I wasn't even thinking. You are right, I should have told you. I feel...I feel terrible that I have disappointed you and Father. I'm so sorry, please forgive me."

Mary raised her chin, squinting at her son. As he looked back into her eyes, she saw her boy had grown, even in the few days they had been apart. He seemed taller, holding his head up high. She noticed a few whiskers sprouting on his formerly hairless chin.

Her eyes softened, and she reached out to touch his cheek. He grabbed her hand and kissed it.

"We need a place to stay for the night, then we'll head back to Nazareth," Joseph said, directing the two shepherds to begin the search.

He looked back to see Mary and their son wrapped in a tight embrace.

"Do I have anything else to wear to the birthday party?" Jesus asked his mother several weeks later as she was cleaning cooking utensils. "I mean besides this tunic?"

"You have that darker one, but that's all," she answered. "We haven't had much money lately to buy you a new one."

"It's six inches too short. They'll laugh at me. Again."

"Again? The young ones have been laughing at you?"

"Oh, it's not a big concern. I see them laughing and teasing all the other kids. It's not that they only pick on me."

She smiled at his answer, knowing he was far older than his thirteen years.

"Why do people laugh and tease each other?" Jesus asked. "I see the sorrow on their faces when that happens, mostly the smaller boys who get picked on the most. Why do they do that, Mother?"

"They're just…people, I guess. Maybe they want to feel more…important…or powerful," she said.

"By ridiculing each other? That seems just so backward to me. I wonder how I can fix that?" He looked off to the horizon like the answer was somewhere out there.

"Don't worry. They're just kids; they'll grow out of it. Eventually. This too will pass."

Jesus made a mental note to remember that particular phrase.

"Now, what about that birthday party?" his mother said after a minute.

Jesus blinked his eyes several time quickly and smiled at her.

"I'll just wear this one. I'll wash it this evening."

"Did you get her a present?"

"I made her a birdhouse. She likes birds."

"Will there be many other children there?"

"We are not children, Mother. Most of the boys already have apprentice jobs. And yes, there will be both boys and girls at this party."

"Oh, sweetheart, your first boy-girl party. Are you nervous? A little, maybe?" she said as she tried to suppress her smile.

"I don't think I understand these young ladies yet, Mother, that's for sure. They seem to be much different from the boys in town."

"You think, huh? Quite observant of you, my Lord." She smiled at her son and dipped her head slightly. It had become a routine between them as Jesus transitioned into a young man and began taking life very seriously. Mary liked to inject a bit of humor to keep him on an even keel.

"Don't start that. I'm only 13. I know I have to learn. And I believe it's your job—and Father's—to help me, right? Not to poke fun at what I will become, just help me get there." He also tried unsuccessfully not to smile as his mother grabbed him around the waist and tickled him.

"How dare you," he laughed, "try to make your Lord and savior giggle like a schoolboy! Now bow down to me."

"You are still not too young to bend over my knee and give you a good whipping, young man," she said as her eyes danced and the dimples on her cheeks spread wide with her laugh.

"You just might do that when you see I haven't yet cleaned out the barn like you asked days ago." His final words were barely audible as he ran out the front of the tent.

When her laugher subsided, Mary clasped her hands together under her chin and smiled at the heavens above.

"Oh, Jesus, I just love it," the young Jewish girl said, turning the birdhouse over in her hands.

"Made it myself. Well, me and my father."

"You're so thoughtful…and caring," she replied, reaching out to touch his hand.

He froze, not sure what to do. He noticed that sweat began to trickle from his armpits down his sides. He wondered if he smelled bad, knowing that would offend the young girl, whom he noticed smelled like sage. Maybe next time, he thought, I should rub a little sage on my body before I go to a party.

"Thank you for coming to my birthday party," she said, bringing him back to the situation at hand.

His hand was still in the grasp of the girl. He didn't pull it away, knowing he needed to understand how it felt.

"My pleasure," he said.

"When's your birthday?"

"Uh…we don't make birthdays a big deal in our family," he shrugged.

"How come?"

"Well, we did once, but…anyway, it's a long story. Better left for another time," he replied.

"Even still, no celebrating birthdays? That must be terrible. I feel so bad for you."

"You feel bad for *me*?" he asked.

"Well, sure, I mean, I guess. Why?"

"Oh, nothing. I'm just trying to figure this whole thing out."

"What whole thing?"

"You know, boys and girls, and…and that whole thing."

She wrinkled her face and withdrew her hand. "I think I'm going to see how they're coming with pin the tail on the donkey," she said as she walked away.

He thought to himself, *This might be a little harder to figure out than I realize. They don't use a real donkey for that game, do they?*

He wandered over to find out.

That evening, Jesus gathered his father and mother together by the fire.

"I have a few questions I thought you could help me with, okay?" Jesus asked.

"Sure, son," Joseph answered. "Shoot."

"Why do my knees suddenly hurt, like all the time?"

"It's probably growing pains," Mary said. "You're growing so quickly your body is having trouble keeping up with your growth spurt."

Jesus thought for a moment. "It hurts to grow? Huh. I'll remember that."

"But if food makes you grow," the boy continued, "is that why we fast? So, we won't grow, and therefore, my knees won't hurt?" A slight smile crept into his eyes.

"You're messing with me, aren't you?" Mary asked.

Jesus's eyes grew wide, and he slowly shook his head in mock denial.

Mary grinned. "Sometimes you are just too big for your tunic."

"Next question," he continued. "Father, as you explain the math of carpentry to me, I understand numbers. But why all of a sudden did you insert letters? It makes math so confusing."

"Well, if you're looking for an unknown number, like the length of the board, the letter becomes a placeholder until you figure it out. I'm sure somebody will think of a name for this method, but now we just call it math with letters. But I can see how confusing it is at first."

"So, what I hear you saying is that when you add more detailed unknowns to an equation—or a story, let's say—it makes it more difficult to understand. Right?"

"Right, but," Joseph continued, "it sometimes makes you think harder and that thinking makes you smarter in the long run. It's like a revelation, and you remember it."

Jesus made a note; he liked that thinking.

"I don't want this next question to sound too vain," the boy said. "But will I ever have a full beard? I'd hate to be depicted for all eternity with just a few scraggly chin hairs."

Both parents laughed out loud, as did the thirteen-year-old.

"On a more serious topic, sometimes I doubt my abilities. Will the father," and here he pointed to Joseph, "not you the father, but the father above, will the father forgive my doubt?"

"*You* have doubt?" Mary asked. "I never suspected that. But I suppose that's the teenager in you. We all doubt at that age. It's natural. It's human to doubt. And yes, I believe you will grow out of that, but remember that feeling of uncertainty as you grow into a man. It will serve you well."

"Thank you, Mother. I am always amazed at your wisdom. I love you so much."

Mary beamed.

"I don't understand this one," Jesus said. "What is the big temptation with fermented wine? All the kids want to try it. They say it makes them happy, but all I see is goofy when they take some."

"Some kids, and some people, don't know the meaning of happiness. And they mistake other feelings for it," Joseph said.

"Oh, how terrible. That makes my heart ache just thinking about it. I'll need to work on that one, won't I?"

Both parents nodded in unison.

"This seems so overwhelming at times," Jesus said, barely audible.

Mary spoke. "Life can be that way. For you, time will help you figure it out, and the father will instruct you. Both of your fathers. But remember, some people will not trust the instruction and will live in overwhelm their entire lives."

Jesus's shoulders slumped, and he looked down at his dirty feet in his worn-out sandals. He didn't speak for several moments.

"When will I be ready?" he finally asked.

"Soon. Have patience. God will let you know when to begin," Joseph answered.

"But Father, I don't feel anywhere near ready," Jesus said, looking at the ceiling of thatched straw. "I don't understand these feelings I'm having. I don't understand why I see so much pain in this world. Why people treat others with scorn and ridicule. Why there is so much deception and lying and just plain evil surrounding us all. It's all so confusing to me. I want to make it right and fair and just, but I have no idea how to do that. Will I ever? If so, when?"

"We've all felt those emotions. Every single one of those feelings," Mary began. "Some hurts just don't go away. We may not show the world how we feel, but that doesn't blunt the trauma of the pain in us. You were meant to feel all those, too. And I suspect you will feel much, much worse. But it is your destiny, your purpose. To absorb it all—all the pain, all the sorrow—and all the evil."

Now a sense of dread spread across the young boy's face as his mouth drooped and lines creased his forehead. He felt his muscles tense and a sharp pain penetrated his stomach.

Jesus wept.

Joseph reached out to the boy and pulled him into a tight embrace. He whispered in the boy's ear, "Do not despair, my son. Do not lose sight of the father's purpose. There will be joy in all the land. That he has promised us. We don't know when it will appear and why you must suffer, as I see you now. But you have been chosen from that very first night when the star appeared. You are the one. The only one who can save us. The one."

Jesus took a deep breath and wiped his nose with the sleeve of his tunic. He lifted his head, pointing his chin, and looked into his father's eyes. He exhaled slowly and nodded once. Then he smiled.

Edict #15

I saw the courier give the signal. It was a simple sign, yet full of complexity. Three fingers across his right eye, sliding down his cheek, and finally pulling on his right earlobe. Now I knew the location and time of this week's meeting, if my memory served me right and the calculations I devised were accurate. It had taken me six months to decipher the signals, and I hadn't confirmed the accuracy of my suspicions. I'd find out tonight. My entire future depended on it.

Then he quickly walked away. He'd given the signal to nobody in particular, just launched it into the tiny space of this corner for anyone to see who happened to be looking. He had his rounds to do, at similar street corners across the city. I'd followed him before.

I knew from my investigation that he never used available mid-twenty-first-century technology. He certainly could have broadcast this message much more efficiently to the hundreds of people waiting for the sign, but they hadn't used technology for several years. Just too dangerous, and there were many people— bad people with horrible intentions—on the lookout for this communication.

When I returned to my apartment, I opened a book on the bottom shelf of my bookcase, turned to page 103 and found the notebook page I had inserted. If somebody happened to find my apartment and see the hundred or so books on my shelf, they would have to check every one before they found these handwritten notes. The special page contained my interpretations of the many signs I had tracked since I started to follow the group.

As I calculated the signs, I confirmed that the group would meet this evening at 3 a.m. at a location they hadn't used before. From my experience of observing these clandestine gatherings from afar, I knew they often met between midnight and daybreak. In today's world, that wasn't so strange. Ever since the Alliance had issued the proclamation—Edict #15 was the official title—groups like these had been driven underground into darkness.

I needed sleep. Tonight, I'd attend my first meeting.

I arrived early, hoping that I'd found the right location. I approached the side door of a rundown building in a deserted part of town. The name of the town isn't important. Mid-sized, a couple hundred thousand people, decimated by the first half of the twenty-first century and its economic collapse. Most all buildings on this side of town were rundown and neglected, and much of the city was deserted as people congregated toward both coasts. A single young man stood outside.

"I'm here for the meeting," I said, trying to mask the tremble in my voice as I approached him.

He looked directly into my eyes, scanned my face, then shrugged. I knew he wouldn't recognize me. They had strict regulations about admitting new people. But I also knew they thrived on newcomers—it was how they worked, how they continued, and how they grew.

He motioned me to the left, down a long hallway. There, another young man waved to me and beckoned me to follow. After we descended a flight of stairs, we entered a dimly lit room with half a dozen young men who all stared intently at me. The moldy basement gave off a pungent smell. I noticed a few card tables and folding chairs scattered about.

One young man politely asked me to sit and offered water. I accepted and drank half the glass. After they wrote down my address, birthdate, birthplace, occupation, and a few other personal details, the questioning began. He didn't bother asking my name; names had become almost trivial in society. I would have lied about it anyway.

"How did you find this meeting?" the blond young man asked with little concern.

"I saw the sign on the corner. I've been tracking those announcements for several months." I decided early on that truth was my best approach—to an extent.

"Do you have friends or acquaintances attending this evening?"

"No. Well...I don't think so."

"Why are you here?" the dark haired, bearded man asked, his eyes never leaving mine to check his clipboard.

"I want to know more," I replied, trying my best to keep eye contact with him

"About what?"

I knew the right answer. I'd done my research. But I didn't want to seem too practiced. I suspected they had ways of weeding out unwanteds, even spies. It had become that kind of world. Never trust anyone, at least to begin with. If I simply blurted out the name, it may seem too rehearsed.

"The man," I finally said, trying to put pleading into my voice. "I don't know his name. Maybe...the Manager?"

Then they all left me and huddled in a far corner of the room. I could hear raised voices and arguments. Finally, one motioned me to an adjacent corner.

I was fingerprinted and eye-scanned, my blood drawn. Probably for a quick DNA check. They walked me to a machine for a full body scan, including facial recognition, and patted me down twice by hand. I was told to wait and make myself comfortable, that it would take a half hour or so. I was positive they wouldn't find any "problems" because my identity had been wiped clean by my organization.

After forty-five minutes, two men warmly shook my hand and led me back upstairs into the main meeting room. As we found seating in the large room—probably a movie theater in its past life—they sat on both sides of me. I noticed the room was only half full a few minutes before the starting time. We sat there for another hour as individuals trickled in. The room was not well kept. Badly worn chairs were haphazardly arranged on the dirty floors. Most of the overhead lighting was dimmed. A large stage fronted the room, and a portable amplifier and microphone on a stand stood alone in the center of it. Black curtains on each side of the stage looked like they hadn't been used in half a century. Visible dust encrusted them.

At exactly 4:00 a.m., a casually dressed middle-aged man with a graying beard approached the mic.

"I sincerely apologize for the late start. We have many new people in our audience this evening, and we needed to...process them. Welcome to all of you," he began, smiling at the crowd.

"I'm the Manager," he continued, and I noticed broad smiles spread across the faces of many in the crowd. Nobody clapped, but many raised both arms in a salute of sorts. He had no notes, nothing in his hands. "You are welcome here, no matter your background or your rap sheet. You will not be judged on anything in your past. Unless, of course, we discover that you're from the Alliance."

Smiles had suddenly turned to masks of concern, maybe hatred. I think I even heard several people growl under their breath.

"If you *are* from the Alliance, we consider you our enemy. We will not try to win you to our side or convert you, as they used to say in the language of the past. You are a threat to our existence and must be eliminated. But enough of that. We have confidence in our procedures and truly believe that tonight we are surrounded by God's love for all of God's people in this building. Tonight, you will be moved by the power of God's word, and you will get an update on how he continues to work in a world that has abandoned him."

Smiles returned to faces.

"I'd like to ask the Historian to please come out now," he said with one arm raised to his left. Almost everyone put their hands together in what looked like prayer.

Carrying his own microphone, an elderly gentleman limped slowly across the stage toward an armchair that had been brought out from the other side.

"Before you begin, Historian, could you bring us up to date on your recruitment and training?" the Manager said.

"Surely. We have twelve individuals in the Historian training. It's a vigorous and demanding routine, and as you may know, not all who enter will graduate. Of the twelve, I will soon recommend those who will continue and those who will work well in our Book Historian positions. For the new people here tonight, these folks will memorize one book of the Story and be responsible to train others in its memorization. We continue to recruit at all levels."

"Thank you. If you have interest," the Manager said, "please see me after the meeting. Now, if you will settle yourself in prayer. Take several minutes. When he is ready, the Historian will recite tonight's reading." The Manager walked off the stage.

Many people knelt at their chairs. I could detect deep breathing. The room went silent. I looked to my right and left. Both men had their eyes closed but weren't kneeling. I sat, stretched my aching neck muscles, and closed my eyes.

I don't know how long it was before the Historian began to speak.

"Tonight, I will speak from Jeremiah, chapter seven. We always recite from the New International Version. Lord, may the words of my mouth and the meditations of my heart be pleasing to you. These are the words of the Lord.

"This is the word that came to Jeremiah from the Lord: 'Stand at the gate of the Lord's house and there proclaim this message:

"'Hear the word of the Lord all you people of Judah who come through these gates to worship the Lord. This is what the Lord Almighty, the God of Israel, says: Reform your ways and your actions, and I will let you live in this place. Do not trust in deceptive words and say, "This is the temple of the Lord, the temple of the Lord, the temple of the Lord!" If you really change your ways and your actions and deal with each other justly, if you do not oppress the foreigner, the fatherless or the widow and do not shed innocent blood in this place, and if you do not follow other gods to your own harm, then I will let you live in this place, in the land I gave your ancestors for ever and ever. But look, you are trusting in deceptive words that are worthless.'"

The old man paused for several seconds. He smoothed his gray beard with a hand gnarled with age. I could see a serene look on his face. Then he continued:

"'Will you steal and murder, commit adultery and perjury, burn incense to Baal and follow other gods you have not known, and then come and stand before me in this house, which bears my Name, and say, "We are safe"—safe to do all these detestable things? Has this house, which bears my Name, become a den of robbers to you? But I have been watching! declares the Lord.'"

The Historian kept reciting, all from memory, with his eyes closed, his radiant facial expressions matching the power of the text. I tried to listen, to absorb, but my mind wandered. Still a novice at listening without seeing the words in front of me, I looked back at how I had reached this point. I trained with my organization for several years before I embarked on this journey. I'd been working now, in secret with few close friends, for—what was it?— six years. It seemed much longer. At times, the loneliness was crushing. I tried to shake away those memories and concentrate on his voice.

"'...When you tell them all this, they will not listen to you; when you call to them, they will not answer. Therefore say to them, 'This is the nation that has not obeyed the Lord its God or responded to correction. Truth has perished; it has vanished from their lips.

"'Cut off your hair and throw it away; take up a lament on the barren heights, for the Lord has rejected and abandoned this generation that is under his wrath.'"

He continued to recite for what seemed like an hour, but I was afraid to look at my watch. Finally, he stopped. The crowd didn't move. A quiet calm had taken hold of the room—and maybe the universe for all I knew.

He whispered into the microphone, "God's word." The room began to stir as people sat back in their chairs, and the Manager eventually returned to the stage.

"Thank you, Historian. Let me remind everyone that these recruits he spoke about will need prayer and both emotional and financial support. This will be a full-time job. Please help them," said the Manager. "Now, let's bring the Proprietor to the stage for his report."

A young man in his early thirties walked out. He held nothing in his hands. He took the microphone and began.

"We have recently acquired another copy of the Story," and this time the crowd began to cheer. He motioned with his hands to calm down. It took several seconds.

"Of course, I cannot say how we obtained it or where it is located. The Historian has verified its legitimacy. That now brings the total to twelve copies of the Story in our possession. We will continue to rotate hiding places and recruit new Locators from our midst. Only I and one other person know the identities of all the Locators. On a sour note, we almost lost a copy last week. Only the magnificent fortitude of one of our Locators prevented tragedy, although the actual Locator had been compromised and has since been shifted out of the area. That person is fine, by the way, and wanted me to tell you that his work is now complete, but he yearns to come back to all of us. It will be several years, but we hope to see him again."

I'd heard that story this week from one of my sources. In the version reported to me, that Locator had been terminated on the spot. I supposed that the Proprietor didn't want that version repeated.

"If you are interested in becoming a Locator, we have several that will be terming out. Please let me know. Thank you, that is my most joyous report." And he left the stage.

The Manager returned and began to speak again, "And now for a short message. It has been forty-one years and 237 days since the Global Alliance issued Edict #15, abolishing religion across the world. To those of us who remember, it will always be the darkest day we will experience in this life on this old planet," he said, looking directly at the crowd.

He moved gracefully on the stage; I could tell he was a practiced speaker.

"For those of you who are new tonight, that might be hard to hear. Forty-one years seems like an awfully long time to wait—for anything. Most of you were not born when that day spawned all that has transpired since. You do not know what it feels like to be free. You see now only secrecy, deception, mystery, and concealment. That is not how we used to live, but we believe we will come to see a New Earth in the future.

"Forty-one years, almost forty-two. But not so long in our history. The Jews waited for what seems like forever in the desert before getting impatient..."

An amplified voice from off stage, the Historian:

"'Didn't we say to you in Egypt, "Leave us alone; let us serve the Egyptians?" It would have been better for us to serve the Egyptians than to die in the desert!'"

"Exodus, right?" the Manager asked.

"Correct. Exodus 14:12," answered the Historian.

"So, we must continue to be patient and follow the Lord. Now, for us, it has been over 2,100 years since he first came to this Earth. He proclaims he will come again, and yet, we wonder. We grumble. Perhaps you have lost faith. That is understandable. When faith has been stricken from being, how do you hold on? When everything dictates that you must, and should, live without faith, how do you live with it? When you see very little manna from heaven—or any other sign—how do you persevere?

"We don't even know," he continued, "if there are others out there who believe as we do. We have heard rumors, but it has been too dangerous to communicate. We have seen horrible stories that show the Alliance's brutal retaliation against those who have surfaced. We can't help but absorb some of the propaganda—the lies about faith and God and Jesus.

"And we must take some responsibility for the edict," he said, waiting for a reaction from the crowd.

I heard many No's shouted. I saw shaking of heads and even frustrated arms raised in exaggerated gestures.

"For we were not innocent," the Manager resumed. "We lost the right to worship Jesus."

The lady in front of me began to sob. As I looked around, I saw others holding their heads in their hands. Moans were not suppressed.

"You may say that that right was taken away from us, and of course, technically, you would be correct. But what part did we play? Where did we fail to intervene? How did we make our religion comfortable, in our own synagogues, pushing away others? Or at least making it uncomfortable for them to join in? How did we let our worship turn to hate? Or bigotry? Racism even? We split our congregation into a million different churches, each with their own customized gospel. How confusing that must have been to the outside world.

"When religion became war, the world turned away from us. They found ways to belittle us, banish us, berate us, and exclude us. They turned the rest of the world against us, and we…fought back. We proclaimed our righteousness—and drove them further away. We did not confess. We did not bow down. We arched our backs and clenched our fists. We railed against their sin and ignored our own.

"And now we dangle over the precipice. We are the last remnant. If we let go, Jesus may die forever. So, we hang on. Without hope, without confidence, without any assurance, and without vision of a world any different from the one we know. The only thing we have is faith. And right here, right now, it's hard to hold on to. But we must. We can win back the world. I don't know how. Or when. It seems sometimes that all our efforts turn to dust. We have seen our friends die for their faith. We will see more die, too. Maybe we all will die, and that will be the end. Or the beginning. The beginning of the New World. We can only have faith."

He let that last statement linger. He wasn't quite smiling, but he looked serene, like this ominous prediction didn't faze him at all. The crowd grew restless, tense. I looked around and saw concern and fear on the faces of the people I could see. I glanced at the man to my right, the one who was watching me. He was breathing deeply, and I could feel the tension in his body. The heat from him seemed to radiate to me. I feigned sorrow to the man to my left, but he didn't make eye contact. He continued to scan the room, his eyes darting and his head shifting. Large men stood sentinel at every door. Many women—heads bowed in prayer—knelt in front of the stage.

"As daylight approaches, we have one more bit of business to complete," the Manager said. "We always end our gatherings with a plea for security. We don't like to keep our message secret, but we must. Lately, we have seen breaches, we have seen infiltrations. And they are increasing at an unacceptable rate. So, we have taken extraordinary measures to fight back against them."

I tensed, and my throat dried up. Despite the cold temperature of the unheated auditorium, the sweat from my forehead trickled down my temples. My heart rate spiked up.

"Each meeting, we ask if there are individuals in the audience who want to proclaim their faith. Each meeting, we ask if there are Alliance spies among us who want to come over to our side. Tonight, I ask these same questions. Are there? We won't rush your answer; take all the time you need to make a decision." The Manager's voice took on a commanding tone.

Everyone in the audience raised their heads and looked around. They looked up to the balcony for any sign. Then they settled back in their chairs and waited. My eyes met the Manager's, and I thought I detected a slight smile and a nod of his head. That was my signal.

I rose. All eyes turned to me. The Historian and the Proprietor were now on stage, staring directly at me. As I looked around, I saw that I was the only one standing. I knew I had to confess now.

"I am an Alliance employee." I spoke into the microphone handed to me. I felt the men on each side of me grab my wrists and clamp down.

"Let him speak, without restraint," the Manager said. The men let go, but I sensed they were on high alert.

I continued. "I have been a spy for the Alliance for six years. My job was to find Christian units, exactly like this one, and report back to headquarters and help arrange for their elimination. I found three such units in the past four years."

I felt palpable hostility all around me. People shook their fists, faces were etched in worry and scorn, and several hustled to the doors, ready to escape.

"I first met your Manager about a year ago," I said. All eyes shifted to the stage, but the Manager's smile spread across his face. "I sensed he was an important operative in the organization of this area. I made friends with him, lying about my past and my purpose. But from the start, I also sensed that he knew more about me than I knew about myself, much more. He has that way about him."

I began to relax. I could feel the tension leave my shoulders.

"I don't remember exactly when I told him of my allegiance to the Alliance," I said.

"April 17th," the Manager said from the stage. I nodded.

"I have been working with him ever since," I concluded, drained now.

"Ever since April 17th, I have called this gentleman Paul," the Manager said. "In June, I hired Paul to work for me. He has been feeding the Alliance false information and evaluating our security. I believe in his faith for our mission."

I still saw confusion in most every face I scanned in the audience.

"Paul, would you like to come onto the stage and give us a report of how we can become more diligent in our mission and ways we can keep our mission alive as long as we have to?"

I nodded, smiled at both men on either side of me, and headed for the front. When I reached the stage, the Manager gave me a long hug, and took several steps to the rear of me.

"I know I don't have to tell you all this," I began, doing my best to control my breathing with a deep pull of oxygen. "But the purpose of the Alliance is to eliminate all religious 'movements' as they call them. Christianity in the U.S. is their main target. But...and this is a huge but...I believe they're failing."

I let that statement linger and saw expressions of wonder—and some doubt—sweep the audience. People murmured to themselves or those close by.

"I was a key member of the West Coast infiltration group, and we met regularly three or four times a year to discuss plans and strategies. A small segment of every meeting was a presentation by a prognosticator who would estimate the rise—or fall—of any religion. It's like market research, what's going to happen in the future. They believe—" I looked around out of habit as I revealed the secret, searching for other spies even though I knew none existed in the room. "They believe that they only have ten to twelve years to eliminate Christianity before the movement will be too strong to have any chance to squash it."

Now I saw real hope on the faces in the crowd. The Manager nodded his head vigorously and raised a fist of triumphant power.

"That's the good news," I said.

"The gospel!" shouted a young woman in the front row, her eyes wide in excitement.

"The bad news is that the Alliance will put all their power into eliminating this movement in the next decade—and we'll need to up our game of concealment and secrecy to avoid that. It's gonna get worse before it ever gets better."

"We are built for storms," the Manager said to the crowd, keeping his eyes on me.

"That may be, but you might not realize the power of this storm," I said. "It will be my job to prepare us all for the wrath that they'll bring. I have many ideas right here," I continued, pointing to my head, "to change the way we operate to ensure we'll make it. To ensure Christianity won't die. To give us our best shot to rise again."

The Manager stepped forward, calming the crowd. "Now, who wants to hear the details?"

The crowd rose as one, all hands raised.

Kol Yahweh

I didn't want to go to the weekend meetings. Actually, I dreaded them. I'd been to every single one of these meetings over the past three months, and I'd seen very little progress. Hash and rehash, going over all the same scripture verses, all the same arguments. I saw no way out. No compromise, no solutions.

We'd been meeting in the large boardroom of our church. The elders had handpicked twenty-four of us to meet weekly, every Wednesday night starting at 7:00 p.m. They didn't give us a timeline or a deadline, but we were three months into the process, and although we'd made some progress, the slog felt slow. I had previously served on the prayer team, the fundraising team, and was known in the church as an honest, straight-shooting businessman—with a heart for Jesus. I guess I fit their profile, so I was asked to join this select team. I was now having my doubts.

I mean, I tried to be flexible, to understand what the concerns were, to look at the Bible through new eyes for a new generation. Our church wasn't progressive or anything like that. We are a sound, bible-teaching, conservative church tucked away in a small town. Okay, we're located in California, but that doesn't mean we're whacked out, new age, Kumbaya-singing hippies looking for a new way to interpret the age-old truths of Hebrew traditions.

But our lead pastor told us we faced perhaps the biggest issue the church would need to address in the twenty-first century.

And I wanted to run as far away from it as possible.

Homosexuality.

Can't we just let them do what they want to do, and we'll

love them despite their sin, and…well, just continue to ignore it? I didn't say that, but I sure thought it, all the time. Why bring it out into the open, discuss it as a whole congregation? Because, he said, people are hurting and when people bleed, we respond. That's what we do.

But I'm not a responder kind of guy. I'm more the type that hides in the weeds. Sure, I'm involved. I tithe (mostly). I pray. I lead a small group and attend services regularly, like three out of four a month. I do my part. But our pastor, bless his heart, doesn't back away from challenges, he embraces them. I envy that in him, but it didn't make our job any easier.

I became a part of this group that was tasked with recommending "corporate guidance" on the subject of homosexuality in our church. We were instructed that consensus was not an option. We needed to find unity. Part of the charter of the group explained that we were not a democracy, where majority rules. Not even two-thirds majority was going to cut it. Unity. Like everyone and all. I thought that's what consensus was, everybody in agreement, but I came to understand that there was a distinct difference in the terms. Consensus meant that dissention could be alive but squashed in favor of agreement. Unity meant that was no dissention.

At first, I didn't understand the concept. In the past, on certain issues—especially those that cropped up in life and were not explained in scripture—we'd agree to disagree. Or at least not slam the other side's view. We didn't talk or preach politics, red/blue, right/left, donkeys or elephants. We didn't argue if Jonah could really survive three days in the belly of a huge fish; we focused on God's relentless pursuit of him, even if he was hiding in…well, the belly of a huge fish. We had people in our church who were sticklers for the letter of the biblical law and others who were much more concerned with just loving people, whoever they were, whatever they did. It was a good mix. Until it wasn't.

We let the divide of viewpoints and opinions and interpretations linger underneath the surface. Our people weren't dissuaded from discussing sensitive issues, but the church didn't take an official stance, except for the essentials. And sometimes those essentials—if you didn't take a look at our statements of faith that we hid away on our website—became fuzzy, background, like scenery you can miss if you're not looking. It made our church an attractive place to worship. We didn't really include everyone, but we didn't turn anyone away either. But the dichotomy of trying to be everything to everybody festered to the point that sometimes we didn't take a stand when one needed to be taken.

Our pastor decided that we needed to put a stake in the ground on this issue.

This weekend was the culmination, the come-to-Jesus unity smackdown of those three months of meetings. I guess we did have a deadline after all. Our leaders had taught us all the various details of what would help us be successful: being quiet, listening without interruption, meditating on God's word, praying specifically and passionately, fasting, and letting go of ourselves and letting God lead. That last one seemed to be the biggest hurdle for many of us—yes, me included—but several in the group helped model that behavior. I'd first agreed to be a member of the group because I often felt I was too stubborn to learn from God's leading, and I knew I needed to learn that—however difficult it might be.

We spent those months listening for the voice of God, *Kol Yahweh*. Sometimes putting a phrase into the original Hebrew language gives it more gravitas, more reverence.

As I sat in my car this Saturday morning, I looked back at the last two days. As a group, we'd met on Thursday evening for four hours in that same stuffy boardroom where the stale smell of coffee lingered. All we did was pray. No speeches were allowed, no preaching within the prayer tolerated. You know those kinds of prayers, right?

"God, please take these biased, harmful attitudes (*their beliefs*) away from people in this room. Fill them with grace and gratitude (*because they don't have any now*). Humble them so they can see the right way (*my way*)." It's easy to get preachy in prayers.

Praying for hours on end is hard work. Long stretches of time, maybe a minute, pass without anyone saying a word. Okay, maybe a minute isn't long in the whole scheme of life and lifetimes, but when it engulfs a room and pressure mounts to break the silence, it seems like seconds morph into hours.

I thought Friday night's session—another four hours after a not-so-light dinner of home-cooked burritos—would begin to focus on the solution, the unity, the deep discussions, the revelations, the confessions, the remorse, the hardlines, the scriptures, the triumphs. No, all we did was bless each other. That took me by surprise. The pastor led an evening of anointing with oil to symbolize how each one of us has a heritage, a lineage, a right, and a duty to and from God. Have you ever been blessed like that? With oil and a cross painted on your forehead? I hadn't.

It pivoted the whole evening away from separation and individualism and turned it back to…yep, unity. We're all in this together, the whole is bigger than the sum of the parts, the mosquitoes on Noah's boat were just as important as the lions. I felt a tremendous lightness enter the room, a fading away of self and a surrendering to God.

Now, as Saturday morning dawned and after bagels and cream cheese in the foyer, we settled into the main sanctuary, and the pastor spent thirty minutes recapping the work we'd done over the past months. He'd already distributed the summary reports prepared by the notetakers during the sessions, so we knew the gist. But in his own words he voiced both sides of the argument, including scriptures and other relevant resources we'd found.

The sanctuary space had been reformatted to a small, tighter grouping. The interlocking chairs now formed semi-circles facing the front where a small podium stood sentinel with the pastor slowly moving about the space.

He opened up the discussion for any "final revelations" as he put it but hinted that we needed to be brief and concise without restricting us too much. He subtly let us know that we'd spent enough time on the deep discussions, revelations, confessions, and all the rest. Now, would we find unity in this? Would we be a loving, Christ-centered church that accepted everyone—even homosexuals—that loved everyone equally, without judgement or condemnation, exactly as they are, exactly as God made them? Or…wouldn't we? Would we head in the direction that a very few people in the congregation had expressed to him? To cast the homosexuals out and only allow them back in if they conformed to strict Biblical teaching.

The room was silent. Only a shuffling of notes could be heard. A stifled cough punctuated the silence.

An elder spoke first. "Maybe there are passages of scripture that reflect the timeless will of God and others that reflect God's will in a particular time—but not for all time. And maybe, just maybe—I'm not one hundred percent sure on this—there are scriptures that merely reflect the cultural and historical circumstance in which they were written but never reflected God's timeless will."

"That's blasphemy," said an older man in the back row. From my view, he didn't have unity etched on his weathered face. More like contempt.

The elder nodded. "You may be right. Or it might just be prophecy. I'm not sure myself."

The older man: "The Bible is God's word, inspired by God, 'God-breathed' as if he were directing the words through the hands of the writers, word by word, book by book."

The elder took a deep breath and let it out slowly. I could see his chest expand again before he spoke. "I agree. But they were also written by men. And God shows us time and time again throughout the Bible, starting with Adam and going to Abraham and David, and…and, well, every single man until Jesus, that men are fallible, fallen. Maybe the Bible reflects that prejudice that men inserted into scripture for their own sinful purposes."

The older man squinted his eyes in doubtful scrutiny but didn't say a word.

A middle-aged woman, the mother of four grown boys I knew personally because I taught them all in Sunday school, stood next. She twisted the scarf she had removed from her neck and swallowed twice and wet her lips before she spoke.

"If we allow this...this...to happen in our church, we have succumbed to tolerance." She said the last word in three distinct syllables, her mouth puckering like she was spitting out the sour seed of a lemon. "We have released our standards, we have taken the road of the world, and I shudder to think of what might be next, what we will tolerate next. It's a very, very slippery slope indeed." She sat down with a thump.

John, a plumber and perhaps one of the nicest guys I've ever met in the world, stayed seated but replied, "Haven't we done that already? What about divorce? The scriptures are pretty clear about divorce—as clear as it is about sexual sin—'anyone who divorces his wife and marries another commits adultery.' Pastor, do you want all of us who are divorced, me included, to stand up?"

"I don't think that will be necessary," the pastor said, trying his best to swallow his smile.

"Two wrongs don't make it right," came from the back of the room.

"I'm not saying that," John said, looking for the voice. "I'm just saying that times change, customs change, laws, circumstances, society. Everything changes."

That silenced the room until a middle-aged woman who sang in the choir said, "Just because everything changes around us does not mean that we must change, too."

Then Maggie, the church secretary, slowly rose from her chair. She straightened her back and raised her chin, just slightly, almost imperceptibly. "In my most humble opinion, if you—I mean, if we—read the Bible literally, we could conclude that women have absolutely no business being a part of church leadership. Pastor's preached on that several times," she said, smiling at the pastor. "Wear hats, keep quiet, no shiny jewelry, right?"

"And yet we crossed that threshold," she continued, "of allowing…no, embracing women leaders in our church decades ago. Who in this room—anyone? —would deny that we are a much more compassionate and grace-filled church because of it? Anyone?"

Nobody spoke. After several seconds, Maggie raised her chin just a bit higher, nodded once, and sat down.

That little soliloquy made an impact on me. I'd heard those sermons Maggie was referring to, but the way she expressed it so simply and distinctly allowed me to see that issue through her eyes. Not the pastor's, not mine. Hers.

Next, David raised his hand, and our pastor acknowledged him. David is known as *the* Biblical scholar in our church. He stood at the end of the front row with his Bible open.

"Before you begin, David, let me remind you and everyone else," the pastor said, "that although I would never resist the reading of scripture in a setting like this, we have spent time studying and discussing every relevant passage pertaining to this subject. You all can refer to the list we handed out last month, and Maggie's done a great job of jotting down relevant comments that have been voiced since then in some of our open discussions. So, do you have new insight—because I know you often do after your study—of a passage?"

"I do," David answered.

The pastor nodded to proceed.

"We have been advised by the scripture writers—and God," he began with a genial nod and a smile to the older man who spoke about blasphemy, "that we should refrain from this 'shameful behavior' of homosexuality. And in several places this behavior is detailed, graphically. The first chapter of Romans is perhaps the most vivid picture painted by the apostle Paul. And we all are familiar, I think, with the rather loathsome environment of society in first century Rome. But I want to make two very interesting points I discovered in my research about that time and place."

Here he waited several beats to build interest before he continued. He pulled out a worn notebook and opened it to a place marked by a paperclip.

"At that time in Rome, scholarly, pompous Roman statesmen of good standing, like the elitist class they most certainly were, would often convince the unsuspecting parents of young boys to hand over, for a small fee, those youthful minds for teaching and training. Very noble of them, right? Except as part of the training—after months and months of indoctrination by the self-righteous to obey and respect their elders—these elders would sexually abuse these young innocents."

He let that sink in, and although people rustled in their seats, he had their attention. Several looked away from him, and the silence deepened before he spoke again.

He continued. "The second point concerns the brutality of the Roman soldier of the era, the conqueror. It is recorded that these ruthless warriors would often ravage a village and pillage and plunder to their black hearts' content. They would often leave one more brutal message to deter any future resistance to the power of Rome. To completely humiliate and plunge the final blow of conquest deep into the soul of the conquered...they would rape...the men of the village. Oh, I'm sure they raped the women, too, but can you imagine the utter fear of hopelessness that must have resulted when they abused the men in this manner? Those men must have felt buried alive.

"Perhaps when Paul speaks of such shameful behavior, he was referring to these satanic rituals that Rome had thrust upon the known world for hundreds of years. He just may have...left out some details in his letter because his audience would have already known the connection."

Again, silent contemplation consumed us all.

The pastor, by now, had established a pattern of moving throughout the room like a shepherd circling his flock. He noticed a young woman who I believed to be in her early 20s. Rebecca had her head between her legs, her hands gripping the sides of her chair so tightly the pastor could see the strain and the white of her knuckles. She rocked ever so slightly.

He came alongside her and gently laid his hand on her shoulder. She jerked her head up. Her eyes showed both fear and fierceness. The pastor whispered so that only the few folks who surrounded her could hear.

"Do you have something to say, Rebecca? Now would be the time…if you do."

She nodded several staccato times and stood. I could see the deep breaths she inhaled, as if the air contained something more than oxygen. Courage, maybe?

"Thank you in advance for your grace and understanding," she began as she looked down at her hands.

"You all know, I think, Jenny and Russ Brown's son, Will. We were an item." Now she had raised her head and a slight smile crept into her countenance. "I tried to love that boy. No, no, that's not right. I *did* love that boy. It's just that…. Well, he had the most gorgeous…well, um, let's just say that I believed he was gorgeous in every single way. You know what I'm talking about, right? But I wasn't…attracted to him. I wanted to love him in every way possible, but I couldn't. It wasn't me. I was much more attracted," here she paused for another shot of oxygen courage, "to his sister, Beth." The smile left her face, and she seemed to be looking off to a distance most in the room couldn't see.

"I'm gay. And this is the first time I've admitted that except to a few close friends and my parents." Tears began to stream down her face. "Some girls take pride…gay pride, I guess, huh…in that identity. I haven't gotten there yet. I still feel…guilty and ashamed. I've asked God for years, and I do mean years, at least since I was about eleven, twelve maybe, to take that away from me. Fervent prayers. Heartfelt, like my very life depended on it type prayers. And I suppose it did…does. But I got no answer."

I saw several heads nod in agreement. I suspected that reflected the acknowledgement of prayers unanswered. Right then, the room seemed to soften around the edges.

"I know, I know," she continued, "sometimes he doesn't answer in my time, only his, and sometimes what he answers we can't see or don't want to, and sometimes I know maybe I'm praying for the wrong thing, and maybe I haven't prayed enough…or whatever, but it doesn't seem like that and it doesn't seem like I'm praying for the wrong thing…." She wiped the sleeve of her sweatshirt past her nose. A handkerchief appeared out of nowhere, and she grabbed it without looking or stopping.

"I don't want to be gay. I really, really don't. If you could see some of the expressions on your faces right now, you'd know why that's true. I want to be married to a nice boy, and I want to have children and bring them up in this church. I want a dog and a house and a fence around it and love and marriage…and a very normal life. I've wanted that all my life. All. My. Life. And now I see that it may never, ever happen and that's like…my whole life…disappearing."

I saw several people grab for a tissue and felt the formation of tears in my own eyes. I really didn't want to suppress them, not in this time and place. Not in front of Rebecca. Not in front of God. I now knew why I'd been asked to join this team. I was a fence-rider. Right in the middle. I couldn't—or didn't want—to make up my mind. Like a lot of us in the room, I suspected. But the time for indecision had come and gone.

"I've asked God to change me, make me new, reborn," Rebecca continued. "But He hasn't. And I'm still hurt and ashamed, and I feel all this guilt, every second of every day. But it's me. Maybe I'll never change. I feel like I don't belong…to anyone, to any world, to *either* world. And somehow, someway, I still have to make a life. I have to live. I want to do God's work in this world, and I have no earthly idea how to do any of that now. None. But I know God loves me. He hasn't abandoned me, has he? He doesn't do that, right? We only abandon him, and I will never do that. So now what do I do? How do I survive? How do I make a life that's pleasing to him? To you?" she said, waving her arm across the room.

"To you?" Her pleading eyes focused on the pastor. "To my parents? To anyone?"

She didn't sit. It sounded to me that she was done. That a huge cloud had lifted from the auditorium. But she didn't sit down. She just cried, with the tears sprinkling her sweatshirt, not trying to dab at them or control them. She looked directly into other people's eyes, at least those who would look at her, often through their own tears.

I noticed my breathing had almost stopped. I had to force myself to make my lungs work again.

I'm not saying that the clouds outside suddenly parted and a beam of sunshine burst upon the room and haloed this young woman. Nothing like that, c'mon now. But something had shifted in the room. Something had left, and something had entered.

Then Jeremy, a medical doctor in his mid-forties I suppose, raised his hand to speak.

He stood and smoothed his beard and mustache by stroking it back into place. At first, he looked like he wasn't going to talk. He'd opened his mouth several times, with a breath, but nothing came out.

Finally, "I don't like the direction I think this is going. But I know what I like doesn't have much to do with making this decision. I like giving shots because I know it helps people heal, but I don't know many people who like to get them. I like ice cream, but I know it's not very good for you. So, like or dislike aren't good indicators. I'm trained in my profession in analytical, diagnostic methods, and I've done my best to analyze this…well, I don't want to call it a problem. This situation."

He rubbed his hands together, looking down at them, like

they cradled his next thoughts. I figured he was going to tell us more about doctor analytics.

"And yet, analytics often miss the impact of what the heart tells us. Our heart, our center if you will, can reveal a depth of...feeling, emotion, love even, that our minds cannot or will not grasp. And yet this is not just an emotional decision either, is it? We all know emotion can lead us astray. I have this sense, in this case, that emotion, or love, will win over analytics, but...."

He rolled his hand in the air as if trying to will his next words out of the air. "I'm conflicted. I see the need to accept all human beings into the church. To never ostracize or expel or push away anyone. It's not my job to fix anyone. Wow, that sounds very strange coming from a doctor, doesn't it? And...*and*...I see the need to keep our standards, our doctrine, our inheritance intact. To be the beacon, the light, to a dark world.

"Not that I mean," and here he looked at Rebecca, "your world is dark. It simply may need more light."

She shrugged and shook her head.

"And I guess I need more light, too. I hope you will love and support me as I continue to seek more guidance on this from the Lord. Or until I hear directly from him. I think that will happen. That he'll speak to me. But he hasn't yet. I think maybe some of you have the sense of his leading. Until I have that sense or he opens up another way—which he can do, too—I hope you'll show me the love I can feel in the room today."

More conversations peppered the rest of the morning, and then I thought we'd break for a long lunch—to talk and discuss and pare off into smaller groups. To make a final decision, in unity, to embrace all God's children. But by early afternoon, no lunch.

At two o'clock, the pastor returned to the front of the room and smiled at the crowd. "Thank you all for your role in today's session. And all of you do play a very important role in this room, in this church, and, if I can be so bold to say so, in this world. It's always God's guidance to do good in the world, *for you* to do his work. Sometimes we just don't know what that is or how to do it. Right?"

"You've heard me speak about this before—of how we can use the Bible to seek God's direction. I don't believe we should look at the book like an encyclopedia, searching out facts to support a decision or looking for a specific answer to a question. We have to sift through all the traditions and interpretations and stories for a theme, a tone, a nature and character of God through Jesus to look for the larger messages."

He wasn't really in his typical preaching mode, I noticed. He sat on a high-backed chair and talked to us like we were in his living room. He used no notes, and I often felt he looked directly at me when he made a point. I thought most of us in the room felt the same way.

"We want so desperately, as C.S. Lewis comments," he continued, "to see the unrefracted light that shines on one ultimate truth, and we want it to be a simple formula that can be tabulated, like a multiplication table. But that's not that way it is, is it? God makes us work a little harder to understand. What we do know, what we can bet the house on, is that what God has done—not merely *what he has said*—is what's best for us. The challenge, of course, is to determine what actually God has done—and of course, what he's doing."

He rose and grabbed for his thermos. Sipping, he let that last statement settle into the room.

He continued. "I've used this example many times before. Did God order the destruction of all the Canaanites—men, women, and children—just to show his power, his anger? Or was that someone's interpretation of what they thought God was saying they should do? Do we know, for certain, God's intention, by plucking a verse or two from the encyclopedia and stamping it as God-approved? Makes you think, doesn't it? I hope it does."

Now he moved around the semi-circle to his right and stopped beside Rebecca.

"I'd like to thank Rebecca for voicing what hadn't been said before. For stepping out on the ledge when it might have seemed dangerous, or at least costly. But forging ahead anyway. I hope you'll stay in this church, Rebecca. To help us. Maybe we can help you, too. We need your voice, now more than ever. Maybe you'll be the guiding light to show us the way. Youth and inexperience are never a deterrent to God. He uses all his people for his purposes. I believe you can show us love and grace and forgiveness where we haven't seen it before. Or maybe where we didn't show them to you before."

"Over the past several months," the pastor summarized, "I've seen a softening."

I felt a little bit better knowing that I wasn't the only one who sensed softening. I felt even better realizing that I'd softened, too.

"Not like a muscle softens when you don't use it, but more like a heart softens when you do," he said. "Maybe we haven't reached complete unity yet—we'll find out in a minute—but I think Doc's plea for love and support brings us that much closer to it. Thanks, medicine man."

Jeremy waved his hand in acknowledgment.

"Just a couple of final thoughts before we ask for a show of unity…well, I'll tell you what I have in mind on that in just a sec. We mustn't let this issue divide us or define us. The Presbyterians and the Methodists have fought long and hard on this issue of inclusion of all people, and it's continued to fracture those denominations, even more than they have been before. In fact, to the point that they readily admit they've spent more time arguing than doing God's work. That's why I've asked for unity on this matter. I will not let this divide our church. Some may leave our church—and I understand that. But others will come. We would hate to lose a single soul, and we'll accept any soul that we…gain. Keep in mind, the world is watching us—maybe not this little church in this little town, but they're watching. They want to know if we are a loving, accepting community or a *country club for believers*. That's just my term. Whether what we preach about Jesus on Sunday, we practice about him on Monday.

"Do we love everybody? Or just a small, select few who follow all our rules and regulations?"

He let that last comment simmer as he slowly paced in front.

"Now, let me explain what I mean by a show of unity. Ready? Here are the questions. If you can answer yes to all of them—every single one—please stand. Do we open our doors to all people? Do we declare that we love and accept everyone, including homosexuals? Do we give them all the rights and privileges of this church? Do we not hold back any of our love from them? Do we become a beacon of light in this world to lead the way? Do we?"

I stood first, almost before he voiced the last question. Ten others stood in unison. Then one by one—slowly, like the second hand of a clock moves when you stare at it—each person rose out of their chair. Jeremy, the conflicted doctor, stood. The old man claiming blasphemy didn't smile, but he stood.

We all stood. Except Rebecca. She sat in her chair, head in hands, crying. Then the pastor and Maggie came up alongside her, locked arms, and gently raised her out of the chair.

Killing Lazarus

Although the crowds gathered throughout the day, they grew bigger in the evening. With the fieldwork finished and the dinner meal complete, they would come to his home. They wanted a glimpse of him—Lazarus.

To them, he meant miracles, life.

They also grouped at his grave, where the stone had been rolled away. They'd heard the stories. How he stumbled out in his grave clothes. Stinking of four days dead and yet, somehow, walking and talking.

To the others, he meant death. Not his but theirs.

The others of Bethany also met in the evenings. Some were secretly sent to the home of the "magic man" as they called him. They observed, talked with the crowds, asked questions, and preached. Because they always preached.

The rest of their clan gathered at the temple and contemplated their demise. The topic they most discussed was this Jesus character. This blasphemer, this charlatan. He seemed to be everywhere and on everyone's lips. If he continued to grow in influence, they wondered how their influence would be compromised or negated or cease all together.

"Where is the imposter now?" the chief asked, using the name they had decided to call him.

"We cannot find him," another answered. "Maybe he's in hiding. Perhaps up in the hills. We are not equipped to seek him out up there."

"Have we made any contact with his group of followers?" the chief wanted to know.

Heads swiveled around, each looking at one another but no one spoke.

Finally, one of the others answered in a quiet voice. "We are making progress. We have indications that one of the followers is in need of funds. He is their treasurer and is known in the area as one who is less than honest. We have approached him, and he has shown interest. We may have to sweeten the offer a bit to secure him, but he is susceptible. We believe that we are on the right path, and that the plan will be put into action very soon." He bowed slightly as he finished his report.

"I expect daily updates," the chief said. "Do not let this go unattended. This should be your top priority, above any of your daily duties. Even above your work in the temple. Do you understand?"

Several nodded, and the grimness of the situation was reflected on their faces.

"Let us move on to the next order of business. What do we know of this Lazarus?"

One member of the others, the one who held jurisdiction over the area where Lazarus lived, raised a hand, ready to speak.

"He is brother to Martha, who is a mere laborer. His other sister is Mary, one of the women who follow the imposter. Every time we have seen him, we have seen her. I have it on authority that she is a compromised woman. Probably servicing the entire lot of them. Perhaps a whore."

"Is she part of his inner circle?" the chief asked.

"Not as the twelve but definitely a confidant."

"What has the magic man accomplished since this hoax has been perpetrated?"

Another one took the lead, "He has not had to work since the hoax," he said. They'd agreed never to call it a miracle or a resurrection. The people would only hear that they believed it to be a mere magic trick. A ruse devised by the imposter to grow his power and fool the locals. They defiled the eyewitnesses by tarnishing their character and shaming several into recanting their stories. They started rumors that many of the witnesses had received payments in silver to deliver the story.

"How, then, is he surviving?"

"They bring him food and other supplies. He accepts it all."

The mood in the temple room turned dark. Each man was lost in his thoughts, looking down at the finely carved wooden table. Finally, the chief stood and paced the small chamber. He lit a white candle and bowed his head, as if in prayer. He'd been thinking of the next move in their power play to regain command. His time in this territory had taught him that the Romans were not a patient group. Whenever they saw weakness, they pounced. They had obliged this small group of others to keep control of the people who had come to the temple to be taught, but the chief knew that if he lost this upper hand, the Romans would be swift to yank control from his group and perhaps even destroy the temple.

"This magic man is a threat. He must be eliminated," he said, still facing the wall where the candle flickered. "Perhaps if he died, the imposter would lose much of his power. That could be a blessing to us."

"Wouldn't the imposter just plan another hoax to bring him back to life?" one of the others asked.

"This time we would see that he stayed buried," came the grim reply.

"But how can he be eliminated? He is surrounded all day by these crowds who have come to touch his cloak," another asked.

They talked among themselves in hushed tones. In three small circles of men, they devised plots and hashed plans without consideration or boundaries of good, evil, or in-betweens.

After much talk, the chief replied, "We have reached consensus. We will arrest him—we can figure out the charges later—and bring him in for questioning. If we keep him in jail for a length of time, his followers will have no contact with him, and the magic will fade like the setting sun. Prepare to approach the jailer with our plans. We will need a show of support, so recruit several locals to promote our strategy. I want this to happen well before the Passover, which could overshadow this. We want all to know that deception and magic will not be tolerated."

Planted rumors spread throughout the district. Lazarus was depicted as a liar. It was reported that he had reneged on his taxes. He absorbed taints that depicted him as gluttonous and a freeloader, a leech on society. His reputation in the community became sullied by all kinds of accusations, none substantiated, but many believed by the susceptible. It was not a hard sell; many were eager to believe that he was merely one of them—not magical, not favored.

A small group of envious were paid to protest that the accusations against Lazarus be dealt with swiftly. They gathered around his home and demanded action, protesting against all who gathered to gander. Six Roman guards, on the take from the chief since his elevation to his position, answered the call for justice, or whatever word they used to justify grabbing the magic man. Lazarus struggled against the rude treatment of the two Roman guards who manhandled him into the chamber of the temple. The others had gathered, the chief seated in the chair of power.

"Why am I here?" demanded Lazarus.

"Because you are a liar and a cheat. A blasphemer!" decried the chief.

"That is untrue. It is all untrue."

Suddenly, one of the guards punched Lazarus in the stomach, doubling him over and knocking the wind from his lungs. He slumped to the ground on hands and knees and tried to breathe. The other guard delivered a knee to the head, and he crashed to the marble floor. A third blow knocked him unconscious.

"Throw him in jail," the chief boomed to the guards.

One of the others chimed in. "We must keep this secret, or the imposter may try to free him with another magic trick."

"No, we will tell the people of his imprisonment. We will show what becomes of blasphemers and liars," the chief countered. "And perhaps the imposter or his troop will appear to help their friend Lazarus. Then we will have him."

After several days, news of Lazarus spread among the Jews. A small group, those immune to the heavy-handed tactics of the others, assembled in front of the temple and demanded an audience with the chief. For a day, their complaints were ignored. But they persisted, and on the morning of the second day, the chief emerged from the temple, flanked by a cadre of others, the six Roman guards, and the Jewish police.

"Why is our friend Lazarus under arrest?" a Jew shouted.

The chief quieted the crowd with his hands and waited for the clamor to subside.

"He has perpetrated a hoax. He has deceived the people. He has sided with the evil one. He must be punished," the chief said.

"I saw him die. I saw him buried," one Jew shouted. "I saw him walk out of his tomb."

The crowd chanted their approval. Again, the chief waited for quiet.

"We also have eyewitnesses who dispute that claim."

"Who are they?" the crowd demanded.

"To reveal their names may put them in jeopardy from the looks of your protest today." He said nothing else.

"How long will you keep Lazarus in jail? What is his penalty?" the Jew who had assumed leadership of the crowd asked.

"That will be up to the courts," the chief said.

"But this is a religious dispute. They have no jurisdiction over us," the leader countered.

The chief looked at the Jew with unmasked disdain. He gripped the silver in the pocket of his robe and tried to squeeze out his anger. The crowd sensed his wrath and finally hushed so that his next words could be heard.

"Do not protest this arrest further. We are now looking for accomplices for this deception. You do not want to be implicated," the chief said.

The not-so-hidden meaning packed power, and the crowd slowly dispersed, although with grumbling, shaking of heads, and outright anger.

Two of the others couched in a corner of the square, turned their faces to the wall, and talked quietly so no one could hear.

One said, "What if the Jew leader is telling the truth?"

Doubt flashed across the face of the other. "I have been thinking similar thoughts myself."

"What if Lazarus did return alive from the grave?" the first one said.

"We would be doomed."

"Perhaps, perhaps not."

The clandestine meeting broke up, both men afraid to think aloud about the possibilities one way or the other.

Later that day, the chief gathered his cohorts in the jail to dispense more silver and to set a strategy.

"How long will we keep him in jail?" the lead guard wanted to know. "If his case comes before our masters, anything can happen. Most of it bad for us. And you. How long can we keep him here?"

The chief raised his hand, as if in thought. He paced along the crumbling stone floor, a sneer spreading across his face. Lazarus moaned from his cell and rolled over on his back, spitting up blood, the prior beating—and a second and a third—having taken a toll.

"Not long," he answered. "Look at him. I don't think he'll last long at all. If he indeed was brought back to life, it doesn't mean he'll live forever."

The Carnival Chemist

An allegory about discovering & using spiritual gifts

So, since we find ourselves fashioned into all these excellently formed and marvelously functioning parts in Christ's body, let's just go ahead and be what we were made to be, without enviously or pridefully comparing ourselves with each other, or trying to be something we aren't.
—Romans 12, The Message

Prologue

The assignment made me smile. Doing a series on spiritual gifts, my church opened up one-time small groups for a six-week study. I drew an assortment of young marrieds and singles to the group I would lead. Many were newly married, still in their twenties, and few had children yet. It had been a long time since I was that age or in that stage of life.

From working with this age group before, I knew that most were still immersed in the bliss of being married or they faced that uncertainty of looking for their "one true love". They all were working hard to establish their careers, and many were contemplating the joys and burdens of starting families and having children.

I was a little surprised they signed up for a course on spiritual gifts. At that young age, introspection often takes a backseat to getting on with life. In our first meeting, after introductions and finding out about each other, I asked everyone to write down a couple of their spiritual gifts.

"But we haven't even discussed what gifts there *are* yet," one member of the class remarked.

"Take a guess then. This isn't a test. It's just to gauge where you are in the process," I replied as I handed out 3x5 note cards. "No peeking in the Bible."

During the ensuing discussion, I discovered that several in the group knew gifts like prophecy or evangelism—the big ones— but nobody attributed any gift to themselves. Nor did they know many of the lesser-known gifts. Babes in the woods.

The church planned more formal evaluation of spiritual gifts and talents for anyone in the congregation who wanted to participate. It would be a five-week process in which we evaluated ourselves and then asked others who knew us to also evaluate us. Then several trained elders would hold discussions with each member who signed up in order to "score" all the data and evaluate what it meant. Eventually, I knew the church would attempt to match a spiritual gift with a need in the church and encourage people to get involved in the church based on their gifts. If members worked where they were gifted, they were less likely to burn out.

But many in my group were just trying to understand Christianity—what it meant for their life, how to stay committed to it when it seemed more people in our society were heading away from religion, and how to make God and Jesus real and relevant in their lives.

During the second week of the study, a Sunday sermon explored spiritual gifts and discussed related scriptural references. When my group reconvened, questions bombarded me fast and furious.

"How do you know what your spiritual gifts are?"

"Does the Holy Spirit deliver them or are you born with them?"

"How many does a normal human being have?"

"Can some people really speak in tongues?"

"If you have a special gift, do you really have to use it? What if it's

scary, like prophecy or healing?"

"I know some people are blessed with evangelism, but that could never be me, could it?"

"Can you actually develop a gift, if you think you have it?"

And the questions just kept on coming. I did my best to answer them without confusing everyone. Several in the group were quiet. When I pressed them, they admitted they weren't sure they had any spiritual gifts at all.

The evening was about to come to a close, and the waters were murkier than when we began—I hadn't cleared up much at all. Even though I preached patience to the group, I realized I needed a basic way to look at spiritual gifts that everyone could relate to and remember. Something that would give a foundation on gifts without restricting the group to memorizing long scripture verses or taking extensive surveys, tests, and evaluations.

They needed The Story. The Story of The Carnival Chemist.

Stories were key to Jesus's ministry. The woman at the well, the boy who ran away from home and returned, the marriage reception, the man at the gates of hell. Stories were easily remembered and could be passed down from individual to individual and from generation to generation. If the story was done well, it held attention. But some of Jesus's stories needed detailed explanation, like the "Parable of the Talents" in Matthew. And the church had included that one in its workbook for this study. In Jesus's day, talents were a denomination of money. The parable illustrates how wasting money is similar to wasting spiritual gifts and talents.

As we were about to end the evening, I asked the group to read several scripture passages for the following week, but mostly I wanted them to pray for openness, understanding, and guidance. I told them they would hear a story that had been passed down to me from my father, a pastor, and that had guided me my entire life. They had tons of questions, none that I answered. They left inquisitive, alert, and excited about what the week would bring and what "The Story" would reveal.

The following week, as they filed into the room for the session, I wore a purple pointed wizard's hat adorned with stars and a pair of Crocs. I asked for silence and led a short prayer, asking the Holy Spirit to guide and direct us and to open us up to new learning.

Then I told "The Story."

The Story

Jesse Jennings steered his worn-out Prius back onto the freeway, but he didn't really want to head back to the office. He'd spent his lunch hour staring at his turkey sandwich and wondering if he'd make it through the week. He was a salesman for a teetering company. Ever since the Great Recession, they hadn't made their monthly sales quotas and had suffered through three layoffs. As the sales manager of a small group of salespeople, Jesse desperately wanted to be the best salesman and deliver the biggest numbers, but orders were hard to come by these days.

His two major clients had suffered themselves and weren't buying anywhere near what they once had. Not only that, but before the recession he was sole sourced with both clients, meaning they hardly ever sent orders out to bid to other competitors. No more.

Now the biggest order in several years from a new client loomed ahead. It could make or break the company. If Jesse landed the order—the decision was to be made next week—it might give the company enough business to survive. If he lost the order, the company might fold. He knew they were consistently losing money, and it didn't make much sense to keep on losing it. They may well go out of business.

The prospective new client had been receptive to Jesse's sales calls. They gave him a chance to bid on the job and even relented when he practically demanded a second chance to present his concepts to them. Next week before the big decision was made, he would deliver his final presentation. His last chance.

Jesse did his homework on the company, the products he was presenting, and had practiced his presentation repeatedly. But he'd lost a lot of orders over the past couple of years, and he wasn't sure he had more than a 50/50 chance of landing this one. He worried constantly about the possibilities and the consequences. His competition on this order would be ruthless, promising almost everything and slashing prices to the bone.

On his way back to the office that day, he glimpsed a billboard on the freeway announcing that the county fair was in town and he could gain access at the next exit. He quickly decided a few hours at the fair might be just the remedy he needed to get his mind off his troubles. He pulled off the freeway and headed toward the festivities. The sign above the entrance gate read: *The 2015 County Fair, A Carnival for All Ages!*

That weekday, the fair wasn't crowded. Young families with moms and kids and a few teenagers were about the only visitors. Jesse paid his admission fee and wandered past the booths lining the entrance corridor. Cruise lines, solar companies, t-shirt shops, hats for sale, and stroller rentals beckoned. He averted his eyes from the hawkers and headed toward the midway, the section of the fair with games of chance.

He tried his luck throwing softballs at kewpie dolls. He'd lost a little velocity off his fastball over the years and a lot off his aim. Then he pitched coins at glassware, not really caring if they landed or jumped out. He shot a few baskets at a hoop that seemed taller and smaller than a normal one and missed all five shots. Just the way his week was turning out.

Wandering down the midway, he stopped in front of a small, inconspicuous booth with what looked like a hand-painted sign pinned to a curtain just beyond the booth barrier.

The Carnival Chemist: Mixing Potions to Remedy All Your Troubles

An old man in a purple costume—Jesse immediately thought

of Dumbledore in the Harry Potter movies—sat on a stool in the corner of the booth. He was reading a book and didn't notice that Jesse had stopped. He sported long, white hair down past his shoulders and a white, scraggly beard. As Jesse peered closely, the hair and beard actually looked real. He inched closer for a better look. The old man's clothes consisted of a flowing, faded purple robe to the knees and baggy pants of the same color. His feet were propped up on the bottom rung of the stool, and Jesse thought he recognized a pair of green Crocs.

Just then the old man raised his head and looked directly at Jesse. His eyes were intense but not threatening.

"Nice shoes," was all Jesse managed to say.

"I saw so many kids and grownups wearing them, I had to give them a try. Most comfortable things I've ever owned."

"They go nice with the costume, too."

"What costume?" the old man asked.

Jesse pointed his finger at the man and swirled it in a circle, indicating his clothes.

"Oh, this? It's what I wear all the time. Comfy."

Jesse smiled and nodded his head. He liked the old guy.

"What brings you by?" the man asked.

"Just spending a little time at the fair, an extended lunch break."

"Yeah, I figured. That suit and tie is not typical fair attire. Comfy?"

Jesse looked down at his clothes. "Not really, no."

"Try the Crocs, they're wonderful."

Jesse laughed out loud—for the first time in a long time. It felt good. He didn't want to leave the booth. The old man had returned to reading his book, and Jesse thought it odd that he didn't try to get Jesse to buy something like all the other carneys. Oversized and old looking, the book was bound in intricate leather and could have at least a thousand pages and weighed twenty pounds, Jesse guessed.

After several seconds, the old man looked up and asked,

"Anything I can help you with?"

"Like what?" Jesse wanted to know.

"Like the sign says, I make troubles disappear."

"I'm not sure you could make this one go away."

"Try me. I'll let you know if it's beyond my reach."

Jesse told him the short version of his dilemma and the upcoming sales presentation.

"What else?" the old man asked.

"What do you mean?"

"There's something you're not saying."

Then Jesse admitted that if he didn't make the sale, the company could fold.

"Aha, now I understand." The old man leafed through his book, turning the pages as if he knew exactly where to stop. Nodding his head, he read the page where he had landed, tracing the words with his right index finger, and mouthing a few words, but saying nothing aloud.

"I have a perfect potion for that. Are you interested?"

"How much?"

"Five bucks. And it comes with instructions."

"Instructions?"

"Yep. This is a one-pager. You need to read and follow the instructions exactly before you take the potion. Pretty easy."

Five bucks. What did he have to lose? "Sure, I'll bite."

Once again, the old man looked into Jesse's eyes and held the intense gaze until Jesse looked away.

"It'll take me two or three minutes to mix it up. Stick around or come back in a few."

"Okay, I'll just wander on down the midway," Jesse said as he began to walk away the booth.

"Money up front, please," the old man said with a smile.

Jesse chuckled and handed him a five-dollar bill.

When Jesse returned to the booth, the old man stood waiting for him. He handed Jesse a miniature mason jar about two inches tall with a red wax seal on top. Jesse inspected the glass, illuminated by the bright red liquid inside. He held it up to the light and saw little specs of something inside, which caught and reflected the sunlight, almost glowing.

"What're those little things inside?" Jesse asked.

"Sorry, trade secrets," the old man said.

"It's okay to drink, huh?"

"Remember," the old man said, handing Jesse a sheet of what looked more like parchment than paper. "Read the instructions and follow them exactly before you take the potion."

His skepticism rising, he cocked his head and smiled at the old man. The parchment was handwritten with an old-fashioned fancy script, with big, swirly letters starting each paragraph. It was a little bigger than a typical sheet of paper and included a numbered list of instructions after the opening section.

"Trust me. It'll work."

"What do I have to lose?"

"You have much to lose," the old man said, "and you know that. So, trust me. Read and follow the instructions exactly. They are self-explanatory; you shouldn't have any questions. But if you do, I'm here all day. And all night. When you land the sale, come back, and I'll tell you one of the secret ingredients in the potion."

"Really, you will? The trade secret?"

"I give them away all the time," the old man said.

Jesse turned and began to walk away.

"Remember, read and follow the instructions. Exactly," he heard the old man say once again.

After dinner that evening, Jesse withdrew to his home office to read the instructions. The opening paragraph said:

Read, follow, and complete the entire set of instructions on this page before swallowing the potion. Do this at least twenty-four hours before you want to achieve the result requested.

Jesse glanced at the numbered set of twelve instructions. The first instruction read:

#1: *Know and use your strengths in life.*

I guess I'll have to spend a few minutes writing those down, Jesse thought. Then he continued reading the instructions, estimating how long each would take. He had only four days before the big presentation—and since he was playing along with the wizard—he wanted to make sure he completed them to meet the twenty-four-hour deadline. Then he stopped at the final instruction. It read only:

#12: *Pray*

Jesse didn't quite understand that one. It wasn't detailed. It didn't say who to pray to or what to pray for. Pray to God? Jesse had never done that in his life. Well, that wasn't quite true. He'd prayed several times during his mother's terminal illness, and he prayed when his son was in the hospital with pneumonia. He didn't think that praying twice in his life really counted to God. Would God even know who he was if he prayed? Jesse didn't think so.

He worked late into the night, beginning with instruction #1. He rose early the next morning rejuvenated, and during breaks at the office, he kept working on the set of instructions the old man had given him. He asked several of his office mates to confirm his answers for his strengths—and they even added a few he hadn't thought about.

Instructions #2-#11 took him the remainder of the day, and a full two days before he was to ingest the liquid, uh, rather potion, he came to #12 again. He had googled "how to pray" so he had at least a flimsy idea of what to do. Over the next two days, he prayed.

Exactly twenty-four hours before the big presentation, he

broke the seal on the mason jar, took a deep breath, and swallowed the red, shining liquid. Jesse was surprised that it didn't have a strong taste, other than being a little sugary, like slightly sweetened iced tea.

The following day, Jesse energetically presented his products to the prospective client, using all the strengths he had written down in the set of instructions. He tried to close the huge order right there and then, but the client said they wanted to think about it for a day or two. He left the office with a strange feeling that he may have upped the odds from his earlier estimate of 50/50. He felt good, knowing at least he'd given it his best shot.

Later than evening, when Jesse checked his email for the last time before heading to bed, he froze at the sight of an email from the prospective client. His heart began to beat quickly, and he hesitated just a moment before clicking it open. It simply said:

You got the order. Congratulations! Please contact us tomorrow for details. We look forward to working with you.
P.S. Your high level of customer service was the deciding factor!

Oh my God. Oh…my…God!

Jesse kept repeating the OMG chant for what seemed like five minutes. Even though it was already 10:30 at night, he called his company president and told him the good news. Then he woke his wife.

He barely slept the entire night. And he never once thought about the old man and his potion.

The following day when he returned to his office from his new client with a purchase order for over one million dollars, his office staff threw him a party, complete with a cake and a short speech from the president. Somebody asked him what he'd done differently to land the order, and that was the first time that Jesse thought of the set of instructions on parchment paper the old man had given him. Too embarrassed to mention his visit to the county fair, the instructions, or the potion, he simply said he'd used all of his strengths to the best of his ability.

As the party broke up and Jesse accepted congratulations from almost everyone, a young woman from accounting approached him and gave him a little hug. She whispered in his ear: "I bet you prayed a little, too, didn't you?"

"You bet," Jesse replied. More than you'll ever know, he thought to himself.

On the drive home that evening, Jesse's phone rang through the hands-free device in his car, startling him out of his bliss over the big sale.

He saw that the call came from his wife, Abigail, and he clicked the pick-up button.

"Your son is in jail!" she blurted out, her voice trembling.

"What?!" he replied, a little too loud.

"For selling marijuana," his wife said, barely audible above the freeway noise.

Jesse shook his head, not understanding a thing his wife was reporting. His son arrested? For selling drugs? His son, Jeremiah? Jesse got the address of the police station and said he'd meet his wife there in twenty minutes. On the way, he called his friend Mark, a lawyer, and asked if he could meet them both at the station. After a short conversation in which Jesse could not answer a single question, Mark agreed to the meeting.

After a few forced pleasantries at the entrance, Mark, Jesse, and Abigail met with the arresting officer for about thirty minutes. The young officer told them only sketchy details of the case, but she offered little comfort or compassion toward their boy.

Abigail was adamant that Jeremiah not spend the night in county lockup, and Mark explained that Jeremiah would be released to his parents that night, but he'd be scheduled to appear in court to face charges at a later date. Jesse was grateful to have some alone time with his son that very night. He could hardly wait.

Mark, Jesse, and Abigail agreed to meet at the lawyer's office at eleven o'clock the next morning, giving Mark's staff time to investigate the charges and put together a plan.

"At least in California we have much more lenient laws governing the possession and sale of marijuana," Mark commented outside the jail before Jeremiah was released. "And he's a minor with no criminal record. But the amount he had in his backpack will be the determining factor. If he gets a judge who holds him accountable to the letter of the law, he may be in trouble."

Both parents were rubbing their eyes. They squeezed each other's hand tightly.

"Man, you better pray that Jeremiah gets a lenient judge," Mark said as he departed.

Jesse thought about that word again—*pray*—and an image of the old chemist flashed briefly in his mind.

Jesse and Abigail had posted bail for Jeremiah that evening, and he was finally released into their custody. On the trip back home, the mood in the car bounced from disbelief to anger. Jesse wanted to know what the hell Jeremiah was thinking; Abigail simply shook her head and tried to calm Jesse down. Jeremiah sat stunned in the back seat.

After the meeting at Mark's office the following morning, Jesse and Abigail returned home and started their own investigation into Jeremiah's criminal offense. So far, their son had been very tight-lipped about where he got the marijuana and how long he'd been selling it, but at least he was very apologetic and appeared humbled by the whole experience. That was something to cling to, Jesse thought.

Since Jesse had missed the entire day of work, he decided to drive into the office after dinner for an hour or two. There wasn't much more to be done at the house with Jeremiah's situation, but Abigail didn't want him to leave. She felt they could be devising a plan to continue their investigation. But Jesse still had much to do to process the big order he had received. That euphoria surrounding the big sale seemed like days ago but really had been only yesterday.

Jesse worked until 8:00 p.m. that evening, and on the drive home, the sign again announcing the county carnival jumped out at him. Several times over the past twenty-four hours, he'd thought about the old man, the potion, and even prayer. On impulse, he swerved off the freeway and headed to the carnival.

When he paid the entrance fee, the attendant said, "We close at nine!"

Jesse hurried down the midway and approached the Wizard's booth. The crowds at the fair were much heavier tonight, but again, nobody stood in the front of this booth and the old man was seated in the same chair reading the same book.

Jesse blurted out, "Hello," and the old man raised his head and smiled. But Jesse didn't return the congenial greeting.

"I'm in trouble again," was all he could manage to say.

"I'm sorry to hear that. But you did get the big order, didn't you?"

"Oh, right. Yes, I did. I'd almost forgotten. But how did you know...?"

"Then you really must be in trouble because, as I remember, that was a pretty big deal just a few days ago."

"It was. But I can barely even think about that now. And it doesn't seem all that important at the moment."

The old man frowned. "I see. So, tell me, what can I help you with today?"

Jesse took a deep breath and blurted out the story of his son's arrest, doing his best to add in a few extra details about his son and their relationship that he thought the old man would want to know.

After he'd finished, the chemist asked, "How does that make you feel?"

Jesse thought for a moment, "Incompetent...as a father.

Frustrated. Mad." He sighed again. "And sad, very sad."

"I understand. Give me a minute." The old man sat back down and returned to his book. He once again leafed to a page, tracing the words with his finger and mouthing to himself. He nodded several times. Finally, he looked Jesse in the eye with his trademark stare—confidant, knowing, caring.

"I have a perfect potion for that. Are you interested?"

Jesse didn't hesitate this time, and he quickly answered, "Yes."

"Don't you want to know the cost?" the old man asked.

"Five bucks, right?"

"No. This will take me several hours to complete and the set of instructions runs…let's see … seven pages. So, the cost will be $250."

"Wow. I had no idea. I thought the cost would be $5."

"The first potion simply solved a work issue. This one concerns your son's life. Small price to pay, don't you think?"

"I suppose. But I don't have that kind of cash."

"I take credit."

"And the fair closes in about a half hour."

"I don't close. But I see your point. You can pick up the potion and the instructions first thing in the morning. The fair opens at ten."

"Ten it is. See you then," Jesse said, beginning to walk away. *Am I really going to do this? Do I really trust this old man? I must be crazy.*

"One more thing."

"Yeah?"

"Pay up front, please."

Jesse pulled out his wallet and reached for his credit card.

Jesse arrived at the carnival entrance a little before ten o'clock the following morning, first in line. Except on this weekday morning, there wasn't much of a line. In fact, an eerie stillness enveloped the fairgrounds. As he walked toward the midway, Jesse noticed that many of the booths were still setting up and several hadn't opened yet.

When he arrived at the chemist's booth, it stood empty. He shouted a few hellos in case the old man was behind the curtain, but he only drew a few curious looks from surrounding booths. Jesse asked the carney running the booth next door if he'd seen the old man.

"What old man?"

"The one in the wizard-looking booth, right there," Jesse replied.

"I don't pay no attention to that booth. And I don't remember nobody ever being there."

Jesse thought that was a strange answer, so he just wandered back to the old man's booth.

After ten minutes, the chemist appeared.

"Sorry, am I late?" he asked.

"Just a few minutes," Jesse said, trying not to show his irritation.

"It's just that they make the best candy-coated popcorn over there and it's fresh as sunrise this time of the morning. Care for some?"

"No, thanks. I need to get to work pretty soon."

"I see. All business, huh? Here's a little free advice, but you won't find it on the set of instructions. One of those trade secrets I keep bragging about. Ready? Sometimes you need to stop and smell the popcorn."

"I thought it was roses."

"Huh? Oh, yes! Stop and smell the roses. Well, to tell you the truth, I think roses smell exquisite, but I have to admit, this popcorn smells absolutely divine."

Jesse couldn't help but smile. And he reached over to grab a handful of popcorn.

"Good, huh?" the old man said.

"Yummy."

"Okay, now we can get down to business. I stayed up a little late with the potion, but it's perfect. And the set of instructions came out to be eight pages because I added a few things at the last minute. But there's no extra charge. Here you go."

Jesse took hold of a similar miniature mason jar, this time with yellow wax sealing the top of the container. He held it up to the light again and let the sun shine through the yellow mixture. Small flecks of the potion twinkled in the light.

"Same trade secret in this one?" Jesse asked.

"If I told you that I'd be giving away the trade secret, and I already gave one away today," the old man joked.

"Hey, I forgot to ask last time. You said you would tell me one of the secret ingredients in the first potion if I came back."

"Yes, I did. I'd forgotten, too. One of the most critical ingredients in the first potion that I included was self-confidence. That's what makes it so red."

"Self-confidence? I see. You have a big batch of that behind the curtain, do you?"

"I do. I use that one a lot in these potions. Oh, and here are the instructions for the yellow potion." He handed Jesse a similar set of parchment papers. This time they were strung together at the left top corner with a piece of twine.

Jesse saw that they were written in the same handwriting, and as he flipped through the pages, the set of instructions numbered thirty-three.

"Those will take you a little longer to complete, but you're fully capable. But remember, don't take the potion until all of the instructions have been followed exactly."

"These will take days and days, maybe weeks," Jesse said.

"Depends how dedicated you are. I once read *Lonesome Dove* in two days—600, 700 pages, I don't remember exactly. But then again, I really loved that novel. Read all through the night."

Jesse was lost in the instructions, but he couldn't help but look up and grin at the old man.

"Good luck. If you have any questions, I'm here all day. And all night," the chemist continued. "When the situation with your son resolves itself, stop by again. I just might have some more popcorn for you."

Jesse forced a smile and headed for the exit.

Between work and dealing with his son's arrest, Jesse wasn't able to dig deeply into the second set of instructions until late that evening. At first glance, they looked daunting. He flipped through the pages, taking some notes and beginning to build an estimate of how long completion would take. The opening paragraph mentioned that all thirty-three instructions should be completed but noted that the potion could be swallowed as soon as they were—with no twenty-four-hour restriction.

He shook his head and took several deep breaths. His workload had tired him out, and he still didn't believe wholeheartedly in the old man. *Am I really going to spend all this time working with this carney?*

On the other hand, with the exception of only a few, these instructions were personalized to the situation of Jeremiah's predicament and spoke specifically to Jeremiah, Jesse, and Abigail. It was almost as if the old man knew the couple and their son and had designed assignments accordingly. Insights that only a family member could know were included. Jesse made a mental note to ask the old man how that was possible, but he didn't dwell on it. He had work to do. Once he buckled down to begin, it was late in the evening. He read the first instruction:

#1: Know and use your strengths in life.

He referred to his notes from the initial set of instructions for the big sale and added a few strengths for this phase. After working until 3:00 a.m., he laid down his pen and flipped to the last instruction, #33.

#33: Pray.

He thought he might be a little better at praying than the first time, but he wasn't sure. He began to pray and ended up falling asleep in the lounge chair next to his desk.

The following morning, Jesse decided to take the day off, and he asked Jeremiah to do the same with school so they could spend the entire day together. Jesse thought he could knock out many tasks from his list, and he wanted to begin right away.

He and Jeremiah retreated to Jesse's office and closed the door. The set of instructions sat on the desk. Jesse turned to the second number:

#2: *Tell your son that you love him. From the heart.*

"When is the last time I told you that I loved you?" Jesse asked.

"Huh? I don't know. Hardly ever, I guess. Can't remember the last time."

Jesse hung his head, shut his eyes, and tried himself to remember. He couldn't.

"I'm so sorry. I love you, Jeremiah. I've loved you every day of your life."

"Even the day I got busted?"

"Yes, even that day. Sometimes everybody...no, sometimes I...get wrapped up in other emotions, and the love is kind of like...buried. You know what I mean?"

"Yeah, I guess."

Father and son continued to talk about how other expressions of love, like giving gifts or acts of kindness, didn't quite convey the same feeling as actually telling people that you love them. They communicated throughout the day, and Jesse checked off many of the items on the set of instructions. Grabbing lunch at Jeremiah's favorite hangout midweek was a special treat, and they spent a few hours at the park shooting hoops and talking. During dinner, they included Abigail in the conversation about expressing love. Afterward, when everyone was talked out and tired, Jesse embraced Jeremiah in a big, long hug and told him he loved him. Jeremiah returned the sentiment and retreated to his room for homework.

Jesse slept well that night.

Over the next week, Jesse, Jeremiah, and Abigail worked through the set of instructions. Abigail interrogated Jesse about where he got the parchment bundle, but Jesse hedged and said he was working with a "kind of therapist" and left it at that. Every night before they went to bed, Jesse prayed, but after the first evening, Abigail had resisted the prayer session and left Jesse on his own. She was still concerned about this "therapist" and why, all of a sudden, Jesse was so into praying.

Four times over the next two weeks, Jesse left work early to pick up Jeremiah at school to work on the instructions. His son seemed to enjoy the togetherness and rarely complained about spending time with his dad. They sometimes included Abigail, but many of the instructions involved only father and son. Content to let the men work out the situation, Abigail kept close tabs on the legal situation and the impending date with the judge. Several evenings during that time, Jesse and Jeremiah stopped for a burger for dinner; Abigail usually declined when asked to join them. Jesse didn't understand why, and she gave him no plausible answer.

It took two full weeks to complete the thirty-three instructions. Late one night, Jesse went through all of the instructions again and checked his binder full of notes. Satisfied that he'd completed the list to the best of his ability—and exactly as they were written—he retrieved the vial of yellow liquid that he'd stashed in the back of a bottom drawer in his home desk.

He broke the seal and slowly swallowed the potion. Again, that sugary taste dominated. Jesse waited a full thirty minutes—somehow half expecting that something magical would happen—before he went to bed.

For the next several days, nothing out of the ordinary occurred. Jeremiah still seemed genuinely remorseful and humbled by the experience of his arrest. Meanwhile, Jesse had learned much about his son during the whole process. He had both a renewed interest in the problems and pressures Jeremiah faced, but he also resolved to not excuse bad behaviors. Only Abigail backed away from the process. To Jesse, she seemed overwhelmed and despondent, but when he showed concern, she offered little in response.

The court date finally arrived.

This was not a trial by jury, simply a meeting to listen to the plea deal the assistant district attorney would offer. The prosecuting attorney had given the judge the facts of the case and his recommendations. Jeremiah's attorney was present to advise his client and recommend that he take the deal. After all, Jeremiah didn't have much choice in the matter.

The judge listened to the assistant D.A. and reviewed the documentation from the arresting officer—in this case, a school resource officer assigned to the high school. The judge had also reviewed Jeremiah's previous record, consisting only of two driving violations.

The judge continued the meeting with a short dissertation for Jeremiah's benefit on the evils of illegal drugs, including marijuana. He noted that even though California had reduced penalties for possession of small amounts, the drug was still technically a banned substance in the state.

He then listed several mitigating factors that influenced his decision:

- Jeremiah had no prior arrest record;
- Jeremiah was not arrested on school grounds; he was apprehended on a nearby street;
- Jeremiah had in his possession slightly over one ounce of marijuana;
- Although most of that ounce was rolled into "cigarettes," that fact gave no indication that Jeremiah intended to sell

them;

- And, finally, none of the boys who were gathered around
the car and who scattered as the resource officer approached
or who were questioned after the arrest would confess to
buying marijuana from Jeremiah.

"But these mitigating factors," the judge proclaimed, "do not
mean that you are 'not guilty'. Quite the contrary.

"You were arrested with slightly over an ounce of marijuana
in your possession. I cannot ascertain that you had intent to sell,
but I strongly suspect you did. You seem remorseful and
apologetic, but most young people your age do when they are
arrested. You deserve no jail time."

Jesse was relieved but sensed a huge BUT was to follow. And
the judge delivered.

"The law is quite unforgiving: if you break it, you pay the
penalty. So, here is your penalty. First, you must complete a drug
diversion program. Secondly, you shall receive a one-year
probation and be assigned a probation officer. You will need to
report to that officer monthly and submit to urine tests on a
regular basis. As a part of your probation, you will serve 150 hours
of community service, doing work in a legitimate service activity
the court will approve beforehand. And finally, probably the worst
penalty of all for a young man your age, you will lose driving
privileges and your driving license for twelve months."

Jeremiah's head sunk to his chest, and he sighed deeply. Jesse
thought the penalties were strict but fair. Mark had discussed
possible outcomes before the court date with the family, and these
seemed in line with what he had anticipated. At least Jeremiah
would serve no time in a juvenile detention facility.

Mark and the family met afterwards in the corridor, and Mark
detailed the requirements to Jeremiah. He assured the boy that he
had gotten off fairly, but that it was up to Jeremiah to complete
the sentence to the letter. If he did, he would have his arrest
"sealed" when he turned eighteen, meaning that he would have no

criminal record as an adult. Jeremiah was despondent, especially since he'd lost his driver's license, but Mark assured him that other kids his age had tread the path and that it was doable—and in some cases, the community service could actually be fun and enlightening. Jeremiah arched a skeptical eyebrow but said he'd commit to the process. What choice did he have?

Later that day, Jesse and Abigail sat at their kitchen table and decided to modestly celebrate the fact that Jeremiah wouldn't be going to jail. They cooked Jeremiah's favorite dinner—steak and potatoes—and Abigail made his favorite dessert, a Boston cream pie. They talked about the circumstances that led to Jeremiah's problems and brainstormed ways for him to steer clear of the crowd who was influencing him. When Jesse suggested Jeremiah try out for the baseball team in the spring, Jeremiah acknowledged he missed the sport he'd given up the previous year. Abigail came up with a list of chores to do around the house to earn extra cash so that he could spend time at the batting cages until tryouts started. They fished around in the garage until they found their baseball mitts and made plans to play some hard catch the following day.

They also began to talk about Jeremiah's college plans. Abigail had done some research on testing, grades, entrance exams, and other factors in finding a school that Jeremiah could get into and enjoy. They all committed to continuing the research needed to complete the process. As a junior, Jeremiah still had more than a year to bring his grades up. It would be a long haul but just the talk of going away to college and developing an actual plan for his future seemed to buoy everyone, especially Jeremiah.

On his way home from work the following day, Jesse went back to the county fair to thank the old man for his help and give him an update on his son. Jesse immediately noticed the lack of traffic and was stunned to see that the gate to the fairground was closed. A sign hung from the top:

Thanks for a great 2015 County Fair, A Carnival for All Ages. See you next year!

Now what? Jesse sat in the car and reflected back over the past several weeks and the impact the old man had on his life. The company he worked for had teetered on the edge of going out of business, but the big sale had saved them, at least for the time being. The lessons Jesse learned about himself and his sales abilities might keep them in business for a long time to come.

His son's life seemed to be careening way off track before the set of instructions from the old man enabled Jesse to reengage with his son, set a new path, and bring them closer together. They still had much work to do, but the crisis was averted, and Jeremiah now had as good a chance as any other young man his age to chart his own course for the future.

And renewed self-confidence surged through Jesse. He kept reviewing what he'd written down for the #1 instruction on both lists, his strengths. He honestly evaluated himself and didn't list anything that wasn't an asset. When he perceived that he needed to develop a new strength in life, he sought out and worked with those people around him who possessed that attribute. That process had opened up new conversations and possibilities for Jesse's future. He was excited to see where it led him.

But as his business prospered and Jeremiah's life seemed to get back on track, Jesse believed that Abigail was pulling away from him—and he didn't know why. They spent time talking about their relationship and acknowledged to each other how it had suffered, especially in light of the problems at Jesse's work and with their son. They looked at ways they could revive their marriage, but Abigail was noncommittal when specifics were discussed.

They escaped one weekend to spend time alone at the coast, but even then, they struggled to renew the love that had kept them together for eighteen years.

"You've seemed distracted lately, hon, what's going on?" Jesse asked after they'd settled in a quiet table at a small French restaurant.

Abigail shook her head but couldn't look at Jesse. Tears glistened in her eyes.

"C'mon, tell me, please," he pleaded.

"I feel like a total failure as a mother," she said.

"But Jeremiah's back on the right track."

"No, I don't mean that," Abigail replied. "I just totally missed the trouble he was in."

"But so did I," Jesse said as shook his head at the waiter before he got to the table, shooing him away.

"It's my job, my number one job, to spot things like that, and I missed it," Abigail continued. "Even worse than being oblivious to what was happening in my son's life, now...I doubt my effectiveness as a mother. What else have I missed? Where else has he screwed up, and I don't even know it?" She balled both fists and dabbed at her eyes with her knuckles.

"Abbey, we both missed it. We're only human. He's a good kid, down deep; he'll pull out of this. We did the very best we could."

She raised her chin and looked him in the eye. "But that wasn't good enough, was it?" she said, anger flaring in her eyes.

"You put too much pressure on yourself."

"Don't patronize me, Jesse. I really don't need that right now."

Jesse took a sip of water and rearranged the salt and pepper shakers, so they sat side by side.

"When I decided...when we decided...that I should stay home with him," Abigail continued, "my main focus was Jeremiah. Yeah, I know, I have that little accounting business and that's fulfilling at times, but he was job one. For the longest time, I felt needed and important to his life. Now, I'm not sure. I'm not sure of anything."

Jesse simply nodded, letting her talk.

"There are a lot of people that do accounting. Just learn QuickBooks, study all the changes—tax laws, that kind of thing—and get to work. But nobody else can be a mother to Jeremiah. Nobody. That was my job. For the past year, he's been selling dope, and I had no clue. None. I don't trust myself as a mother much anymore." She sighed and stared blankly at the table.

Jesse wondered about his failure in loving his wife in a similar light. Concentrating too much on work—and even helping his son—how had he missed the way Abbey was feeling now?

The waiter refilled their water glasses but slipped away silently without a word.

"I feel the same way about our marriage right now," Abigail said when the waiter left their table.

"What?"

"What have I missed about you? Where have I failed you?"

"You haven't missed anything. You haven't failed me at all," Jesse replied.

"I doubt that. It just seems like we're so far apart. Almost like we're in the same river, but you're going with the current and I'm swimming upstream."

Jesse reached across the table for her hand, but she pulled it away.

"Pretty soon he'll be off to college and he won't need me at all."

"He'll always need his mother," Jesse offered.

She shook her head, and tears came again. She grabbed her napkin and dabbed her eyes.

"I'll always need you, Abbey."

She squeezed her eyes shut and bit her upper lip. Finally, she said, "I doubt that, too."

The following week, Jesse admitted to himself that his relationship with Abigail was in deep trouble. And that he didn't really know how to save it. They had used marriage counseling after they were first married to help define and understand minor issues and that brought Jesse's thoughts back to The Carnival Chemist. The old man's instructions seemed to have worked wonders—even miracles—and Jesse wanted to talk with him again. But with the county fair closed, Jesse wondered how to find him. And he almost felt embarrassed that he was relying on a costumed character at a county fair to rescue him and help save his love for Abigail. Almost.

He called the county fair office phone number he found online but only got a voice message. He left his number but had little confidence his call would be returned. He scoured online and found another county fair in his state, but they didn't list all of the attractions on the website. He called that office, actually talked to a live human being, but she could find no Chemist among the attractions at their fair. She suggested trying the state fair but admitted it wouldn't arrive in the state until early next summer.

Jesse Googled everything he could think of to try and find a website for the old man but came up empty. He queried his Facebook account but got mostly snarky comments back, like: *You're looking for who? Dude!!!!!*

Finally, he went back to look at the second set of instructions to see if there were any clues to locating the old man. The only one he found was #33: Pray. He prayed that the old man would hear his plea and that he would be found.

Nothing happened for several weeks.

Then one morning as Jesse was reading the Sunday paper, he noticed an advertisement for a home and garden show at another fairgrounds located a few towns away from where he lived. Home and garden shows weren't necessarily his cup of tea, but he wondered if maybe, just maybe, the old man had a booth there. The show had opened the day before, so Jesse jumped into his car and drove to the fairgrounds.

At the information booth, he inquired about a booth called The Carnival Chemist but the young girl behind the counter had no record on her list of exhibits. She did say that several new booths were added since her list was last updated and that they'd be either in Hall D or Hall F—probably. Jesse took a map of the show and headed directly to Hall D. Walking through booths consisting mostly of craft booths, home suppliers, and cooking demonstrations, he didn't find the old man. He wasn't in Hall F, either. Dejectedly, he began to wander around the show that was spread out over a dozen similar halls with many booths in the corridors that connected them.

Having missed breakfast, his stomach growled as he passed the food section of the show. He scanned the possibilities and looked for something that wasn't deep-fried or packed with sugar. He had almost decided on a burger when he noticed a sign for kettle corn—popcorn with sugar. That reminded him of the old man's craving for popcorn and steered him to the booth. There was a small line of about six people waiting for the delicacy, and Jesse joined it.

"Converted you, huh?" came a voice from behind.

Jesse turned and saw that the old man, in his familiar purple garb, had settled in behind him.

"It's you. I've been looking for you," Jesse said.

"I know. But don't get your hopes up for this kettle corn. It pales in comparison."

"I don't care. Is there someplace we can talk?"

"Sure, after you buy me some corn, we can go to my booth."

"You *do* have a booth."

"Yeah, they stuck me with all the guys selling solar solutions for the home. Go figure, huh? Me, so old-school, stuck in with all that new-fangled technology."

After buying two bags of popcorn, they headed to Hall G, where Jesse saw the familiar booth and the sign that read:

The Carnival Chemist: Mixing Potions to Remedy All Your Troubles

"How's business?" Jesse asked.

"Always just the right amount. Any more and I'd be

swamped. How's your son doing?"

"Great., They dropped the charges, and he's concentrating on college now."

They talked about the details of Jeremiah's turnaround, and Jesse confided to the old man how much the set of instructions had helped.

"Well worth the price, huh? Told you so," the old man quipped. "Keep that in mind for future reference."

"O-o-o-kay," Jesse said.

"Now, tell me, what can I help you with today?"

Jesse recognized the question and this time was ready with his answer. He talked for fifteen minutes about everything that had happened over the past month or so between him and Abigail. The old man asked several questions, including how it made Jesse feel and all the things Jesse had done to try to mend the marriage.

Finally, the old man retreated behind the booth, retrieved his leather-bound book, and settled down in his chair. Jesse knew not to disturb him as he rifled through the pages, finger moving lightly across the text, lips mouthing words silently. Several times, the old man smiled and nodded to himself.

At last, he lifted his head from the book and proclaimed, "I have a perfect potion for that. Are you interested?"

"Yes, but I suppose I'd better ask the cost."

"For marriage potions, I charge by the year, one hundred dollars."

"What?"

"How long have you been married?"

"Eighteen…years," Jesse replied, his eyes widening in understanding.

"Then the charge will be $1,800."

Jesse was stunned. "Wow," was all he could muster.

"Yep, that's the typical reaction I get. But let's delve deeper. This situation affects many lives. Your life. Your wife's life. Your son's life. And the life of your marriage, which is a separate entity altogether. A bargain, I think, if it works. And as you've seen, my potions work."

Jesse hesitated. And the old man sat quietly in his chair. Jesse's mind went to all the reasons he should simply walk away without the potion. Maybe the marriage would work itself out. Maybe Jesse could figure out a way all by himself. Maybe, maybe, maybe.

"I don't mean to pry," said the old man, "but perhaps your hesitancy says something about your commitment to your wife. Are there other places in your union with Abigail where you don't jump in with both feet?"

Jesse didn't remember mentioning his wife's name in front of the old man but answered the question. "I suppose."

"I see. How does that make you feel?"

"Terrible," Jesse replied, bowing his head. "But I love my marriage, I really do."

"Ah, yes, now I see the problem. Do you love your wife as much as you love your marriage?"

"What do you mean?" Jesse asked, frowning.

The old man nodded his head, "You speak of saving your marriage, yet you don't talk much about your love for Abigail. Maybe you need to decide which is more important to you. Perhaps we should work on that, don't you agree?"

Jesse immediately realized the distinction. He knew he loved Abigail more than anything else in the world, even more than he loved Jeremiah. How had he screwed this up so badly?

Jesse nodded and reached for his credit card.

"I'll tell you what. I'll charge you half now and half when I deliver the potion. How's that sound?"

"How long will it take to make it?"

"About a week. It's very intricate."

"Sure, what do I have to…?" Jesse couldn't finish the sentence.

"You know what you have to lose, and you're not willing to lose it. That's the first step."

"I should return in a week to pick up the potion?"

"Sure, next Sunday, about mid-afternoon. See you then."

"Anything I can do in the meantime?"

"What do you think?"

"Let's see. I can tell my wife I love her—from the heart— and I can pray. Anything else?"

"Those are always the best two. Now, let me get to work. Oh, one more thing. Stay away from the deep-fried Twinkies. Gut bombs," the old man said as he disappeared behind his curtain.

Amid a driving rainstorm, Jesse returned the following Sunday to the home and garden show and plodded his way to the old man's booth. He found him in his chair, reading the leather-bound book.

"Pretty big storm out there," Jesse said as a way of greeting.

The old man looked up, smiled in recognition of Jesse, looked outside, and said, "I love rainstorms. You know, water from rain falls on the Earth, does what water was designed to do, and then much of it evaporates and returns to rain clouds. What a beautiful cycle, the cycle of life. An even better example than that Disney movie with the lion, don't you think?"

"I never thought of it that way. I guess you're right."

"How is work, your son, your wife?" the old man asked, rising from his chair to come to the front of the booth.

"Work is good. Jeremiah still has his moments, but it looks like he's improving and back on track."

"And Abigail?"

"No clue," Jesse answered, averting his eyes.

"I see. Jesse, I find you to be a very smart, adaptive student. If you continue working with the instructions for Jeremiah, he will remain on a better path. No lifetime guarantees—there never are with children—but I have this feeling down deep inside that he will be fine. Life may blow him off course at times, it always does, but he has a good foundation. That can weather many storms. Now, let's concentrate on Abigail.

"I have a longer set of instructions for you now," the old man continued. "They total fifty-five, and it's an extensive, intricate, intuitive, and completely achievable way to save your marriage and convince Abigail that you love her. You do, right?"

Jesse nodded vigorously. "Absolutely."

"Good, just checking," the old man said. "In this particular case, I highly recommend that you take the potion as soon as possible. Then proceed to #1 and work your fanny off till the marriage ship has been righted. You may notice that the waters will get stormy, like the weather outside, before you see the sun again, metaphorically speaking.

"Do not become discouraged," the old man persisted. "Persevere. At all costs. There may be only one or two goals in life nobler than saving a troubled marriage. Any questions?"

The chemist handed Jesse a miniature mason jar with a fluorescent blue wax seal that contained a shimmering blue liquid. Jesse grabbed the heavy set of instructions with two hands, they held so much weight.

"What if I need help with any of these?" Jesse asked, flipping through the parchment pages.

"I am here. Through next week."

"And after that, where will you be?"

"I'm around. I don't know my schedule off the top of my head, but you found me the last time. You can find me again. I like crowds of people."

Jesse hesitated, his jaw tight with worry.

The old man smiled with his eyes. "Trust me. Have I ever let you down?"

Jesse shook his head.

"One more thing."

"I know, I know," Jesse said, reaching for his wallet.

Jesse stuffed the instructions under his coat and the vial in his pocket and immediately trudged back to his car through the rainstorm. Once inside, he wiped the water from his eyes, laid the parchment papers on the seat, and retrieved the mason jar. Unknowingly, he licked his lips, craving the solution that could save his marriage. He hesitated a few moments and relived the conversation with the old man, concentrating on the part about jumping in with both feet. He realized he desperately wanted to save his marriage to Abigail—and show her that he loved her— even more than he wanted the big sale at his company and to his surprise, even more than rescuing Jeremiah in his brush with the law.

He reflected on how much he depended on Abigail. After the courtship and the passion of the first few years of life together, they developed a marriage where each played a distinct role. Jesse was the optimist, the dreamer, the spontaneously playful one. Abigail fit perfectly into the role of the pragmatist. Her accounting background enabled her to depend on facts and figures but not so rigidly as to inhibit her joy. Jesse always knew that although they were not quite opposites attracting, their individual strengths complemented each other.

He depended on her ability to calm him down and settle his dreaming into practical paths. She needed him to help her get her eyes off the page and gaze into an unknown future—and to be excited about it. Jesse loved how he could lift his wife up, and his joy was seeing her capture a vision and run with it.

But in the past week, he realized that even though she claimed she didn't trust herself as a wife or mother, she had always contributed to their marriage. He just hadn't noticed how much. Where Jeremiah seemed to comment on every little instruction and intrusion in his life by his mother, Jesse missed Abbey's input into his. Jeremiah, growing independent, protested his mother's help. Jesse had gotten so comfortable with Abbey's contributions that he failed to express his love for them. Maybe that's why she was pulling away.

Then he peeled the seal from the jar, sniffed at the liquid, closed his eyes, and swallowed it all. It was an elixir to him, a drug he craved. It tasted sweet, like the others, but with more bite, more flavor. He immediately relaxed and realized how much he depended upon the potion. Deep inside, he knew it would work—as long as he followed the instructions exactly. Without leaving the parking lot, Jesse began to read them.

During the next several days, Jesse realized that by simply reading through and evaluating the instructions, he was excluding his wife from the process. He needed to engage Abigail in the work. Instruction #1 was the same as the others:

#1: Know and use your strengths in life.

And instruction #2 was familiar, with a slight twist:

#2: Tell your wife you love her. From the heart.

Instruction #3 told Jesse to:

#3: Tell your wife how you feel—about her, your marriage, and your lives together.

That was hard for Jesse to do. He remembered all the times his wife asked him to express his feelings. She was persistent. An expression of "I'm fine" or "It's hard to say" didn't cut it for her. She wanted to know what she called expressive feelings, like angry, upset, mad, happy, sad, confused, frustrated. She hated non-expressive blather like good, bad, so-so, and, Jesse's favorite, "on a scale of 1 to 10, I'm about a 5."

But Jesse hung in there. Every time he had the chance, he told Abigail how he felt. At first, she barely noticed, only nodding her understanding. Gradually, she became a little agitated and would counter with a harshly said, "Why are you telling me this?" like she didn't care. But Jesse held the hope that she did—because he had to. Sometimes it was all he had to hold.

The next several items in the set of instructions asked Jesse to complete them on his own, without his wife's input. As he read them, he spotted that additional scribblings were added in the margins of the parchment. The old man had inserted encouraging notes specifically for Jesse. For example, during this stretch when he was working mostly on his own, he saw a handwritten note that said:

Don't give up—keep talking to Abigail even if you think she doesn't want to hear it!

And this note, listed in the margin, on the next page:

Make this assignment the #1 priority in your life right now!

As Jesse worked with the papers, he could almost hear the old chemist saying these words. He imagined himself in the familiar booth, all the background noise of the carnival faded away. The old man's voice echoed in Jesse's ears, along with the caring smile and intense eyes.

Several of the items in this section of the list required Jesse to document his thoughts and feelings. He had purchased a nicely bound journal from the office supply store when he was working with Jeremiah's instructions, and he continued using it now.

These specific assignments asked Jesse to reflect on the early days of his courtship and marriage. He began to write, following the instructions, and wrote several pages on why he fell in love with Abigail in the first place and what he loved about her then.

He remembered the initial physical attraction, for sure, but he also listed all those qualities in Abigail that drew him to her. Her intellect—she could talk in detail about almost everything. Her intensity—she had an inner strength that radiated from her, whether she was talking about her career, her education, or her values. He loved her laugh, and although she was sometimes slow to pick up on his humor, when she did, she never held back her exuberance. Just remembering Abigail back then made Jesse beam.

Next, he penned about their life together now—the pluses and minuses, the highs and lows. Finally, he wrote about the future and what he wanted for himself, for Abigail, and for their marriage.

When Jesse hit #13, there was a flurry of handwritten notes scribbled all over the margins, almost randomly:

Give it at least a year.

You can always skip to #55 if you feel stuck.

When you're done with these first thirteen, tell Abigail your answers.

It's all going to be worth it in the end.

Do not become discouraged. Persist at all costs.

Trust me!

Jesse smiled at the last one. He thought how strange it was that he trusted an old man he found at a county fair who wore a wizard's costume and made up potions behind a curtain. *Wow, look how much I've committed to this process,* Jesse thought to himself.

And Jesse knew what #55 instructed: Pray. So, he often did that whenever he felt stuck. He didn't know how to pray or what to pray for, but he simply prayed what was on his heart and it seemed to work. It made him feel more connected to the old man, who he now considered a friend and confidant, even a mentor.

When Jesse read #14, it made him stop, think, write, and wonder. It simply read:

#14: Spend more time in your wife's life—and less in yours.

What did that mean? Jesse supposed it was a way to bring them back together—to show attentiveness to Abigail's interests, longings, concerns. To actually put her above himself. That was one of those foundational principles that he had tried to accomplish during their marriage.

After Jeremiah was born and they discovered he had a learning disability, Abigail wanted to quit her job, but only if she could find a way to continue to use her education and passion for numbers and contribute to the family financially. Jesse encouraged that and helped her establish a small accounting business with a few clients she could run from the spare bedroom. She'd loved helping small businesses and contributing to their success. Even more, she could complete most of the work in the evenings when Jesse took over caring for Jeremiah. Her sense of failure with Jeremiah that she revealed during their time away at the coast took him by complete surprise.

But Jesse also knew that he deserved some of the blame—lately, he hadn't been successful in spending time in Abigail's life. His own life—and even Jeremiah's—had taken priority. Now it was time to put Abigail first. Jesse made a list of things to eliminate from his life, so he could spend more time in hers. It read:

- *Give up alcohol, except a glass of wine with Abigail.*
- *Decrease exercising alone and increase exercising with Abigail.*
- *Get home early from work—at least two days a week.*
- *Go grocery shopping and offer to make several dinners a week for the family.*
- *Watch fewer sports on TV.*
- *Talk with her about her clients instead of talking about mine.*
- *Let her choose the movies we watch.*

Jesse changed his life and became much more involved in

Abigail's. During the workday, he sent texts to show he was thinking of her. He shared with her podcasts about raising teenagers or running a home-based business that he thought she'd enjoy. He shared his dreams for the future and asked about hers. At first, she resisted his involvement. But he persisted, although not insistently, not demanding attention, but with little suggestions, ideas, favors and thoughtful help. Then, she relented, begrudgingly, and included him more.

After six months, nothing much had changed in their relationship.

Jesse worked through the set of instructions and only one remained, #54. It included Abigail, and he was not at all sure she would even want to participate. This instruction made him think back to his wedding day, now almost nineteen years ago. He remembered many of the details of the ceremony, the reception, and their wedding night. But other nuances of the day weren't as clear. For instance, he didn't remember all of the vows he said that day in front of family and friends. The minister, who was a friend of her family's, had pretty much used the standard ones. Honor, obey, sickness, health—that sort of thing. Jesse had been caught up in the spirit of the wedding day and almost overwhelmed with everything it entailed. The vows were simply a small part of the day that had now faded from view. They didn't hold much meaning anymore.

But #54 kept beckoning. And he sensed that Abigail would want nothing to do with it.

Jesse knew that without finishing #54, his set of instructions were incomplete. To stay engaged with the process as he planned how to accomplish #54, he started over again at #1. Figuring that it had been six months since the process had begun, he knew that he would now complete certain instructions differently. He realized how far he'd come since swallowing the blue potion in his car that rainy day at the home and garden show. He spent time reflecting on the changes.

First of all, the process had humbled him. Many of the instructions had demanded that he put his wife first in his life. Her wishes, her needs, and her feelings came before his. As he worked his way through the tasks, he noticed how hard it was to take a back seat to his wife. He had been very independent before he married, and after the courtship, when they settled into life together, his independence often flared. But now he had a set of instructions that enabled him to see when and where he needed to rein in his identity so that either his wife's or their identity as a married couple flourished.

Jesse also perceived that his thinking had changed in the past six months. Before, he thought mostly about himself. Now, he almost always thought about his wife first. When he first began the process, he was forced into that kind of thinking by what he had been instructed to do. Lately, it had become second nature. He often wondered how many times his wife had been disappointed in his selfishness during the first eighteen years of marriage.

Jesse had been changed by those thoughts. Many of his male friends who didn't think the same way faded away. He gradually forged new friendships—or renewed old ones with buddies that liked what they saw in Jesse. A group of men who wanted to improve their marriages organically formed. They met for coffee twice a month on Saturday mornings and mostly talked about their wives and their marriages.

Jesse often shared insights from the parchment papers, but he never shared the actual document with anyone. And he never told a soul—including Abigail—about his encounters with the old man. He kept the parchments in his home office desk, tucked away under old financial statements where they were safe from detection. He never talked to his friends about the old chemist, who over time almost felt like a figment of his imagination. Jesse could still see the kindly face and the penetrating eyes, and when he prayed, he often felt the old man's presence. But he hadn't been face- to-face with him for many months so the intimacy he'd felt with the old man—as he had poured out the problems of his work, his son, and his marriage—had faded. Jesse realized that he missed the old guy. That he would love to see him again—just to give him an update and to harness any new ideas that might be offered.

As he maneuvered his way through the parchment papers a second time, he noticed that Abigail became more available. In the early months, she often made excuses to be away from home, visiting her growing list of clients or the moms' group for troubled teens she'd found.

For his community service commitment, Jeremiah had begun to work with a nonprofit that served underprivileged youth. Abigail dropped him off from school once a week, and Jesse picked him up on the way home from work. On the days that he served, the family conversation over dinner centered around Jeremiah's workday.

This second time through the instructions, Abigail seemed to stay home more and more. Drinks with "the girls" happened only occasionally now. Time at the gym was confined to morning hours so she could be home in the evenings. Nighttime classes for crafts or computer design or yoga gradually went by the wayside.

Jesse and Abigail still had not been intimate in almost a year, but lately Jesse noticed that she would touch him in loving ways. At the movies, she would hoist the armrest between them into the up position and intertwine her arm through his. On long walks, now a regular routine, she often grabbed his hand before he grabbed hers. During dinner prep, as he was cutting veggies or marinating the main dish, she brushed her hand along his shoulders as he had been doing to her for months. It wasn't much and it was never talked about, but Jesse felt her touch and knew in some small way that touch was an important link to repairing their relationship.

Jesse had never been much of a talker in the early years of their marriage, but he took instruction #3 very seriously now.

#3: Tell your wife how you feel—about her, your marriage, and your lives together.

He made it a point to express himself whenever the moment felt right. At first, Abigail reacted suspiciously to the feelings. But over time, she began to smile with a slight eye roll whenever Jesse went into one of his "feelings talks." She would smile and say, "Here we go," when he began. But Jesse forced himself to continue. Now it felt good to get those feeling off his chest, whether they were negative or positive. And Abigail always seemed to enjoy them. Her defensiveness began to subside when she thought he was criticizing her. She gradually began to see her involvement in those feelings and took responsibility for them when the shoe fit. But Jesse never tried to blame her for his feelings.

When Jesse first began to tell Abigail that he loved her— from the heart—she would simply look away. But he knew instinctively that instruction #2 was essential to their marriage. They had both uttered those words early in the marriage, but somehow, they'd been crowded out by day-to-day circumstances and non-attention to details of the heart. They eventually lost the meaning behind the words. But as Jesse reincorporated those feelings into his everyday language, he began to rekindle the meaning. At first, Abigail would not reciprocate. And that was okay with Jesse. Maybe, at the moment, she didn't love him, at least not in the way she had when they first married. Maybe she was distracted, lured away from his love, in such a way that she couldn't clearly see her feelings for Jesse.

When this tended to discourage him, Jesse reread the handwritten notes in the margins of the parchment, specifically:

It's all going to be worth it in the end.

Do not become discouraged. Persist at all costs.

Trust me!

Over time—over a very, long time, Jesse thought—Abigail's response to his declaration of love shifted. From looking away at first, she now kept eye contact when he said it. Jesse felt like she was testing him, peering into him to see if he really meant it. He had to concentrate to hold her gaze. But he did.

Then one day, she answered him with a simple, "Thank you." Not "I love you, too," just thank you. To Jesse, that signaled major progress. Every once in a while, she would answer, "I know." At first, a hint of exasperation clouded her voice, but lately, that had turned into acknowledgement and gratitude. And just last week, during a tearful sequence in one of their favorite movie love scenes, she had whispered, "I love you, too, Jesse. You know that." He almost cried.

But #54 still beckoned, and Jesse wasn't sure Abigail was ready to hear it and act upon it.

One night after a glass of wine, he asked her to complete #54 with him. But she sat up straight on the couch, looked confused and confounded, and then left the room without explanation. As Jesse tried to talk to her in the bedroom, she finally admitted she wasn't ready.

Dejected, Jesse left early for work the following morning and stayed at the gym later than usual that evening. As the couple got ready for bed that night, Abigail said, "Jesse, I'm just not ready to do that right now. I really appreciate how you've changed over the past six months or so, I really do. And I know you love me deeply. I love you, too. I just need a little time to process the whole thing. Will you give me that, please?"

"Sure," Jesse replied.

After Abigail went to bed and turned off the light, Jesse couldn't sleep so he slipped out of bed and retrieved the parchment papers again. Along the border of one of the sheets, he again read the old man's hand-scribbled note:

Give it at least a year.

Jesse checked the calendar and realized that he had met with the chemist at the home and garden show almost exactly eleven months ago to the day. He thought to himself, *I can wait one more month. I can even wait many more months if I have to.* Then he made the determination to not waste the next month waiting for Abigail. He flipped to the page of instructions he was most recently working on and studied it deep into the night.

One evening about six weeks later, Jesse and Abigail walked along a neighborhood hiking path near their home. Abigail reached for his hand and squeezed it gently. Jesse breathed in the smells of the evening—the oleanders and eucalyptus trees. Occasionally, when the breeze shifted, he could smell Abigail's perfume.

Abigail slowed when they came to the view that stretched out over the valley, a favorite spot of theirs to observe God's wonderful landscape. She leaned over and hugged him and planted a kiss on his lips.

"I'm ready," she whispered.

And Jesse knew exactly what she meant. *#54, here we come.*

When they returned home, Jesse pulled out his journal and flipped to the page where he had taken notes on his final assignment. At the top of the page, he had printed:

#54: Rewrite and renew your wedding vows in front of family and friends.

"I see you've already got a head start," Abigail remarked, looking at the journal.

"I've known for several months or more that I've wanted to recommit my life to you, so I started to write down some thoughts."

"I see," she said, smiling. "You knew I'd come around."

"I wasn't sure, but I wanted that more than anything in the world."

"For a long time, I wasn't so sure, Jesse. I thought that we'd lost whatever chance we had to keep our love alive. Then you changed. I don't know what happened, whether it was Jeremiah's troubles or what, but you changed. And it took me a long time to notice."

"At least you finally did."

"There are some things I did in the meantime that I'm not proud of, and I need to tell you about them," she said, looking away.

"Maybe sometime. But not now, okay?"

She only nodded.

"Now, let's work on these vows," Jesse said. "I'm pretty sure mine sound more like '70's hippie talk than real marriage vows. I need your help."

"Let's see them." She slid her hand into his and peered into the journal.

Three months later, Abigail and Jesse renewed their wedding vows in their beautifully decorated backyard in front of forty people. They wrote the vows themselves and conducted the short ceremony without the services of a preacher. To them, it was more personal that way, more from the heart.

Jeremiah was accepted into the college of his choice the very same week, so the family had lots to celebrate. Jesse's company seemed to be doing well, and sales were trending up.

Jesse had bound the three sets of instructions into a heavy, ornate binder he found at a local crafts store. It held a reverential place in his bookcase, and he knew eventually he'd share it with Abigail and Jeremiah. He referred to it almost weekly.

Strolling hand in hand through the arts and crafts show that lined the streets of their hometown, Jesse was lost in memories of the past few years. His marriage to Abigail was better than ever, and they'd joined a small church in the outskirts of town. Jesse now led a men's group once a week that concentrated on making marriages work. Abigail's accounting business was flourishing, and she thought about renting building space downtown and ramping it up. Jeremiah had completed his first year at the university and was thinking about majoring in environmental science. If he could get through chemistry. Jesse had joined a new company and saw his future as almost unlimited. Every member of the family still struggled with life at times, but through communication, understanding, and a little prayer, they always jumped over every hurdle.

As Abigail was admiring the paintings in a large booth near the kettle corn booth, Jesse stopped to glance around. Standing in line at the booth was a familiar costumed character dressed in purple. Jesse approached from the rear and noticed a new pair of Crocs on the chemist.

"I see you finally found those shoes in purple," he said, whispering in the ear of the old man.

Flashing his trademark smile at Jesse, he said, "Like I always say, the most comfortable shoes in the world."

The old man bought Jesse a small bag of the candied popcorn, and they returned to his booth. As the swirl of people all around them hurried past, the old chemist only had eyes for Jesse as they talked for the next thirty minutes. Abigail had texted Jesse, and they agreed to meet at a section of the exhibit with music and a dance floor when he was ready.

"I'd really like to know one of those *special ingredients* in the potion that you promised to tell me," Jesse said.

The old man looked around as if he didn't want anyone else to hear and said, "Goldschläger."

"Gold what?"

"Goldschläger. It's Swiss schnapps. Try saying that three

times. Supposedly, it's got little gold flakes in it. Real gold. That's what makes it sparkle."

"Schnapps? Like liquor?"

"Sorry to disappoint you. It also makes the water a little sweeter."

"*Water?* It's only water?"

"Yep. The power is not in the potion; the power is in the instructions. But I found that some people just needed the potion to make it all work. The potion is really just a placebo."

"You tricked me," Jesse exclaimed, trying not to smile.

"I did, didn't I? But it worked, too, didn't it? So, it doesn't really matter how we got to where we are, just that we got there. Listen, when you were made in the workshop…"

Workshop?! Jesse thought.

"…in the workshop, you were unique. You still are one of a kind. Nobody in the world, who is or who has ever been, was made like you. Your fingerprints are the example most people think of. No two people in the world have the same. You were already made with a 'special potion,' so to speak, so I didn't need to reinvent the wheel. I mixed those potions I gave you with my own hands, and I stirred each and every one with this finger right here," the chemist said, holding up his left-hand index finger. "Yep, I'm a lefty. Whodathunk it?"

Jesse thought about that for a few seconds. "I have to admit, I did feel better when I thought the potion had the power."

"It did have some power. My power." The old man smiled. "Then we're okay, right?"

"Yeah, we're fine. Whether I needed the potion or just the instructions, it all worked out."

"I was very proud of your commitment. To stick to the plan. To see it through. To save your job, your son, and your love for Abigail."

"Thanks. I couldn't have done it without you." He reached out and hugged the old man.

"I get that a lot."

As Jesse was departing, he looked at the chemist and asked, "Will I ever see you again?"

"I'm here all week. And now, you know how to find me if you need me."

Jesse waved goodbye and headed toward the dance floor. When he glanced back, the old man had picked up his book and settled into his chair.

Epilogue

As I finished the story, a hush covered the room. Apparently, nobody wanted to break it to ask the first question.

Finally, a young woman in the back spoke up. "I know this is going to sound like a dumb question, but what did that story have to do with gifts and talents? Sorry, I know, huh, stupid."

"That's a perfect question. Anybody have a guess?" I countered.

One young man offered, "Well, Jesse would've had to use his gifts and talents to get out of all those situations?"

"Exactly. What else?"

"I guess his gifts and talents would have been in the set of instructions some way, like they may have emphasized his gifts," another pondered. "Maybe God gives them to you, right?"

"Right, that's where they come from. God gives you gifts so you can do more than you possibly could imagine. They are a part of him in you, a little bit of God inside each of you. He gives ordinary people just like you and me gifts that let us do things that are so much greater than what we could do without them. Gifts from God make each of you special and unique and so much more powerful."

The group was still a little puzzled about where to go from here, so I suggested a short exercise.

"I listed alphabetically the spiritual gifts that we came up with over the past several weeks. Everybody take a copy," I said as I handed out the sheets. The list looked like this.

- Administration
- Apostleship
- Compassion
- Discernment
- Evangelism
- Exhortation
- Faith
- Giving
- Healing
- Helping
- Interpretation of Tongues
- Knowledge
- Leadership
- Miracle Working
- Prophecy
- Servanthood
- Shepherding
- Teaching
- Tongues
- Wisdom

"My mom said there should be one more," a woman's voice said from the back of the room.

"Oh, yeah, what's that?" I asked.

"Soup making."

The room erupted in laughter.

"No, no, she said it's a real talent and that when you use it, it can solve a lot of problems. It brings people together, it shows compassion, it's helping them stay nourished, and it's serving them. I'm just saying…that's what she says."

"Okay, I like it," I said. "I'll add it to the list. By the way, remember what we said a couple of weeks ago. This list is a compilation, so there could be some different gifts, in different terms—like soup making—that you'll find in other resources. We're just using this list as a guide."

I asked another question, "Looking at this list, what were some of the spiritual gifts that Jesse used that maybe he didn't know he had when he started?"

"How about faith?" a man called out.

Everyone nodded.

"Servanthood!" a woman added.

"Compassion."

"Shepherding."

"Those are all correct," I answered. "Maybe if you had asked Jesse what he thought his gifts were when he started, he would have said something like Administration. As a sales manager he was organized, he could get things done, and he could teach other how to get things done. But at the end of the process, he might've listed all those that you just mentioned. My point is we are bestowed with more than one spiritual gift and we can develop other gifts that may be dormant in us. Gifts we haven't used yet. Got it?"

More and more nods from the group.

"Here's another way to look at spiritual gifts," I continued. "The gifts come alive in delivering them. Yes, God bestows them on us—and we all get a different mix of gifts. But to use the gift, we have to put them into practice. In this story, Jesse obviously had some gifts as a salesman, as a father, and as a husband. But because he got distracted, he slipped away from using his gifts. The set of instructions made him use the gifts he already had. He had to rediscover his gifts."

We then discussed dominant and dormant spiritual gifts. Some in the group were surprised when another person attributed a spiritual gift to them. They hadn't realized they'd revealed a particular gift.

"One way to really uncover all of your gifts is to ask somebody who knows you well to help you discover them. Your parents would be a good start. Or if you're married, ask your husband or wife. If you're in a small Bible study group, that can work, too. Don't you think that Jesse had to enlist the help of others in completing his sets of instructions? Sure, of course, he did. You can't do this all alone. You can't even do it simply between you and God."

"But how would we know that from this story?" one of the students asked. "And why doesn't the story tell us exactly what every instruction was so we could learn them?"

That got a lot of "yeahs" from the group. Everyone wanted to know the answers to those questions. I waited a bit before offering an opinion. I wanted to see if anyone else might offer one. I just raised my eyebrows, encouraging them.

"Maybe each set of instructions is so different because each situation is different," somebody wondered.

"And…?" I added.

"And if you got a specific set of instructions, you might think those exact instructions would work in your case. Or in every case."

"Bingo!" I applauded. "It's not like a set of assembly instructions. Life isn't quite that predictable. It's constantly evolving, and the set of instructions for life has to evolve with it."

More nodding. It was sinking in.

"You use your spiritual gifts and your communication with God to lead and direct you in life. That's why the first instruction was always: *Know and use your strengths in life.* Jesse wasn't spiritual to begin with, which is why it was worded that way."

"Then why was *Pray* always the last instruction. Shouldn't that have been the first?" someone asked from the back of the room.

"Anyone want to speculate?" I asked. Several responses just came bubbling out:

"Maybe if the chemist would have listed it first, Jesse would have

freaked."

"Maybe the old man realized that most people use it as a last resort."

"God can't make you pray or force you to pray."

"Maybe Jesse had to learn to pray gradually."

"Maybe just finding the wizard in the first place was an answer to prayer."

"Maybe the other instructions were a form of prayer."

I only smiled, knowing that the story was producing the effect I wanted. The students were now thinking on their own and coming to understand there isn't always just one right answer to a question.

"And doesn't the Bible say that you really don't have to know what to pray for or how to pray?" I asked. "That God takes your moanings and groanings, your frustrations, your longings, your pleas—he takes that all as prayer. So, as Jesse worked through the instructions, he actually was praying."

"Something else is bugging me about that story," a young man in the group said. "Why did all those instructions cost so much? Would God really demand payment for his help? That just really sounds weird to me. And wrong."

"Anybody see an answer there?" I wanted to know.

"Well, Jesus paid a pretty high cost. To save us. Didn't he?" a woman responded. Others murmured agreement.

"I think if you become a Christian," a man said, "then at first you don't realize what you have to give up to lead that life. But eventually, you do and that's the cost. What you give up."

"Maybe the money Jesse had to pay just represents those costs?"

"And if he'd gotten them for free, maybe he wouldn't have thought they were worth much," one of the women said. "Like 'you get what you pay for,' that type of thing."

Then I injected, "As young Christians, you may not realize yet what all those costs are. That's something to ponder as you continue to grow and thrive in Christianity."

But I had to admit, the students were smarter and wiser than their age might indicate. The story had served its purpose—to get the group to think about gifts and talents and to show how to include God in the process.

"But one more thing I want to make sure you understand," I added. "This is Jesse's story. It's centered in some very universal concerns in the world—job, children, marriage. Many people have those issues to deal with. But it's still just Jesse's story. You have to uncover *your* story. Don't forget that. Some of you aren't married yet and may never marry or have children. But that doesn't mean you don't have purpose or gifts to contribute to the world."

"Next week is the conclusion of the study," I said. "Come prepared with ideas that everyone in the group can use to," I held up one finger, "determine what your spiritual gifts are." I held up a second finger. "And two, how to use them in everyday life." I knew I had their attention as they watched my hand, so naturally, I raised a third finder. "And three, how to develop other gifts that may be dormant right now."

"Maybe we should pray about the whole assignment during the week, too, huh?" a man in the front row said.

The room filled with smiles.

"I think the Carnival Chemist would like that. Just go easy on the Goldschläger."

Author's Note

I'd love for you to use this story and the following discussion questions in a group setting. I know it'll open up new ways to look at and use spiritual gifts. Have fun with it, too. And if you have questions, you know how to reach me.

Additional Questions and Exercises for Discussion

These questions can certainly be pondered alone, but their power comes alive within a group discussion. Resist going through the questions quickly. Each question has depth and could be pondered and discussed for hours.

1. Has God ever appeared to you "in person?" Discuss your interaction with God. How do you view Him? For example, do you see Him as only an ethereal heavenly figure? Does He speak to you in some way? Can you talk to Him in a give-and-take conversation? Does He simply live in the Bible? Do you distinguish between God, Jesus, and the Holy Spirit?

2. As a group exercise, have each member of your small group evaluate everyone's spiritual gifts. Each member could fill out a 3x5 card for every other member of the group, listing that member's spiritual gifts. Spend a few sessions discussing each member's gifts, giving them all their 3x5 cards. Then a spreadsheet could be produced with gifts on one axis and names across another axis so all can see the distribution of gifts among your group.

3. Discuss the list of spiritual gifts noted in the epilogue. Do a little research and see if you agree with all the gifts listed. What other terms are used in your resources for specific gifts?

4. Discuss in the group what could be some of the "missing instructions" in all three scenarios that Jesse faced. Start by discussing big picture ideas for the instructions and work your way down to specifics.

5. How do you keep your spiritual gifts alive? Discuss ways to utilize your gifts.

6. Are there times when you lose sight of your spiritual gifts? When life is tough, do you tend to lose your gifts or use your gifts?

7. Discuss how you feel when you're using your spiritual gifts and talk about how you feel when you're forced to perform outside your gifted areas. For example, if Evangelism is not your gift, how do you talk about your faith to others?

8. Talk about "expressive feelings." Do you use them often? Or do you tend to slide toward expressing feelings like Jesse did at first? Make a list of feelings that express accurately how you feel.

9. What "costs" have you had to pay to follow God's direction for your life?

10. How have you avoided God's direction for your life because you thought the cost was too high?

11. If the leather-bound book in the story represents the Bible, can you find all your answers to your spiritual gifts there? What other resources can you use to supplement the Bible?

12. Discuss "self-confidence" from the aspect of this story. Can God give you self-confidence? If so, how?

13. Do you pray together with your spouse or significant other or members of your family? If yes, what are the benefits? If no, why not? What are the barriers?

14. For married couples and couples in committed relationships: How do you avoid the many pitfalls and pressures of marriage/commitment? Be specific. Are there areas of your marriage when you do not commit completely? Do this as a group and as a couple. Also, how do you renew the spirit of when you

were first married or committed?

15. The Chemist mentions "only one or two goals in life nobler than saving a troubled marriage." What might be those goals?

16. Do you go through periods of your life, like Jesse did waiting for Abigail, when God seems distant or unavailable? How do you reconnect with God? Does God often seem distant in your prayer life?

17. Do you ever think of God making you in his "workshop"? Discuss with others how that makes you feel.

Author's Note

As the subtitle implies, this short story opens the door to discovering and using spiritual gifts. It's not meant to be a comprehensive tool for each individual to find their gifts and put them into practice. That will take a little more study on your part. I hope you embark on the journey and continue to develop your gifts and talents. You might consider reading *The Purpose Driven Life* by Rick Warren as a means to deepen your knowledge.

Here's a snapshot of my journey of discovery so that you can see how I found my spiritual gifts, how I put them to immediate use, how I tweaked the way I serve, and how I continue to find new gifts that God enables me to use for His good.

After accepting Christ as my savior at the age of forty, I jumped with gusto into serving my local church in Northern California. Wherever and whenever I could. But I quickly learned that there are way too many needs at local churches and because I have many gifts and talents—some stronger than others—they were willing to plug me into service areas almost randomly. At first, I was very enthusiastic to help wherever I was needed. But if you serve continually in areas that are not your strengths or that don't use your gifts and talents, it can lead to frustration and burnout. Sometimes you need to serve because the need is so great, but if you serve using your God-given talents, service will rarely result in frustration.

Here's the caveat: I didn't wait to discover my spiritual gifts before I began to serve, but I discovered them along the way. Please remember that. Don't wait, jump in, and discover. Don't spend a long time discovering and identifying; just serve and they will come to the surface for you to see.

I eventually took a class to determine my spiritual gifts and began to concentrate on using my top three. At the time they were leading, teaching, and serving. I say "at the time" because I'm convinced you are given many gifts and with practice, prayer, and patience, you can develop and use more than a couple. Once I focused on using my leading and teaching gifts, I thrived. I joined teams, led groups, even spearheaded areas I knew little about, like fundraising, and as a result found my church life was fulfilling, Christ-centered, and Christ-led.

I then started to use my personal skills—like writing and speaking and marketing—to substantially leverage my spiritual gifts. I supervised marketing projects for the Christian school that the church ran. I wrote marketing brochures and newsletters and helped craft events to increase attendance at the school. I spoke from the church pulpit, the school stage, and in small groups as a part of my teaching. The senior pastor was a master of identifying gifts of his congregation and putting them to good use for the church. I can look back at that ten-year period and say without any doubt whatsoever that God was using me to the utmost of my God-given and life-driven abilities. What joy!

But we moved. And we changed churches. Although I found more niches in which to serve, the next pastor was much better at teaching from the pulpit than identifying gifts and utilizing his people. I had to press—sometimes hard—to use my gifts and talents. I had to step forward. I had to volunteer. I had to say: "I'm good at this. I have a talent for this. Let me do that."

It's sometimes easy to sit on the sidelines. Especially if you've been cranking hard at the church level for many years. Sometimes you need a break. A vacation from service, a Sabbath. And that's fine. Just don't go on permanent vacation.

Six years ago, my wife and I moved to Southern California for many reasons, mostly family related. But for several years prior to that I heard God whispering to me. In my daily prayers, He kept encouraging me to relinquish my hold on a public relations business I was running at the time, and to write more about Him. I ignored that whisper for too long. It's not a great feeling—actually it's a horrible feeling—to believe you hear God's voice telling you to do something—and you're not doing it. I believed I was letting God down. I knew He was saying: "Use this gift I have given you," and I was replying: "Yeah, soon, but I'm using this *other* gift you gave me right now." Let me confess to you—that is not how to respond to God!

In the six years we've been in this part of California, I've written four manuscripts, I've got two additional ones outlined, and recently started to take notes on my next novel. In July of 2016 my Christian memoir, *Lumberjack Jesus*, was published. In the summer of 2019 my Christian novel, *The Resurrection of Johnny Roe*, hit the market. I'm not saying I've found the promised land like Abraham did, just that my time in the desert has been very productive. For one reason, I believe—I heeded the call from God. I stopped ignoring the whisper. I trusted Him and I used the gift He was providing for His purpose.

Here's another caveat: It's always His purpose! You may not frequently hear God's voice directing you, but through prayer, listening and talking with God, you will begin to get an inkling, a tidbit, a tad of what He wants you to do. Then go do it! Jump in. Use those gifts and talents. He will let you know how He wants to use you.

Don't wait until you identify your exact gift, find the perfect situation to serve, and all the stars in heaven align for you to begin. The need is great, and you will learn to serve God in whatever capacity He provides. I believe, after all, that is why we are here, that's why He chose us, that's why we accepted His invitation to accept His Son as savior—to serve Him and His people. So, jump in, the water's just fine.

Santa Barbara
Winter 2020

Author Note #2

This story birthed another book I wrote for parents, to be published soon, with a working title of *American Teen: 33 Strategies to Teach Teenagers Self-Reliance, Confidence and Responsibility.* Keep checking my website, www.bkirkpatrick.com, for availability.

About the Author

Bruce Kirkpatrick spent over thirty years in Silicon Valley as an executive and entrepreneur. Since his move to Southern California, he now divides his time between writing and serving on nonprofit boards of directors, including Christian Education Development Company and Extollo International. His nonprofit work includes helping to train Haitian men and women in employable skills so that they can find jobs, feed their families, and have hope for the future.

His first novel, *Hard Left*, was published in 2007. His memoir, *Lumberjack Jesus*, debuted in 2016. For more information, visit his website BKirkpatrick.com.

CPSIA information can be obtained
at www.ICGtesting.com
Printed in the USA
FSHW010508231020
75154FS